# TO BE HUMAN

## *The Conflict Continues*

# TO BE HUMAN

*The Conflict Continues*

KWADWO GALLMAN

ISBN 978-1-7359749-0-3

Library of Congress Control Number: in-publication-data
Gallman, Burnett, 19XX -


Cover designed by Mia Mack
Back cover photo: Matt Gray,  Radius Images

For information on the content of this book, email
kwadwo@aol.com

WrightStuf Consulting, LLC
Columbia, SC
www.wrightstuf.com


Printed in the United States of America

A Luta Continua!

Buime Kwadwo Gallman

# Dedication

To Listervelt Middleton, my guide, my leader, my friend, my brother from another mother who convinced me that fiction was a viable method of teaching. Even after his untimely transition to the ancestral realm, he has frequently reminded me to get started and has repeatedly prodded me to complete this effort. He was and is more than a friend but an inspiration. Although he still visits, his physical presence is sorely missed.

# Acknowledgments

There are many people whose work has inspired parts of this effort. First of all, many thanks are due to Ayi Kwei Armah for his profound body of work. His **Two Thousand Seasons** and **The Healers** initiated a major change in my life that has been continued by his later works, especially **KMT**. The few days that he spent in my home while on a lecture tour are among the most cherished in my life.

The philosophies, events and even characters in this book, although fictional, were inspired by the work and personages of scholars, friends, teachers, and Jegnoch with whom I've been blessed to develop relationships and for whom I have tremendous respect. Included in this number are Marimba Ani, James Small, Wade Nobles, Leonard Jeffries, Rosalind Jeffries, Theophile Obenga, Charles Finch, Runoko Rashidi, and Tony Browder.

I am also tremendously indebted to the esteemed Ancestors that I have been blessed to know and learn from: John Henrik Clarke, Asa G. Hilliard, III, Frances Cress Welsing, Nzinga Ratabisha Heru, Baba Hannibal Afrik, Kobi Kambon, Larry Obadele Williams, Charsee McIntyre, Jacob Carruthers, Richard King, Anderson Thompson, Patricia Sekhmet Newton and Ankh Mi Ra.

The Ancestors who I have not known personally but whose works deeply influenced me are Amos Wilson, Chancellor Williams, John G. Jackson, Bobby Wright and the Great Pharoah, Cheikh Anta Diop.

I am also profoundly thankful for the work of Na'im Akbar. There are people around me every day who inspire me, who stimulate ideas and who reinforce a comfort zone in which I can not only relax but bask. This is not a small feat when one considers the two wars that Afrikan people find ourselves engaged in simultaneously, the world war and the civil war. The paranoia required for survival can be disorienting, but many thanks to Jodi, Khali, Sterling, Derrick, Joe, Jerome, Ron, Bran, Bill, Seitu, Bennie, Glendora, Norma, and Kwame for helping me navigate those treacherous waters.

# Table of Contents

# PROLOGUE

Obadele struggled to remain calm despite the icy terror that made his mind race and his muscles feel like tightly pulled rubber bands. The chill in the sub-freezing air amplified his terror. He called on all the years of training that had prepared him for just this moment. He was curled in a fetal position, like a partially closed jackknife, laying on jagged, ill-kept pavement on a deserted side street dressed in only his underwear. The predawn hours were deathly silent. The two tall, burly, blue-eyed blonde-haired men, dressed in dull gray uniforms, each built like a thick tree trunk, had been taking turns punching and kicking him. He managed to cover his head with his hands and forearms, blocking most of the blows aimed at his face and head. That was little consolation, however. His ribs, back and abdomen, as well as his hands and arms, were exposed to the thunderstorm of violence. He called on his Ancestors to help him will the pain away so that he could keep his mind clear.

Discovered while trying to get home, back into New Atlantis, he had been stopped just before reaching the rendezvous point in the alley. He had weighed the options of running versus fighting, but the militiamen had been trained well. Although he was confident that he could have defeated them in hand-to-hand combat, they had positioned and spaced themselves in such a way that fighting would have taken too much time. He was just far away from the rendezvous point that he couldn't reach it without being shot. Horde guards were excellent marksmen and loved to kill. So he took the punishment, looking for an opportunity to get away.

The men waled away at him, one beating him with a baton while the other held a weapon on him. The taller man, his long stringy shoulder-length blonde hair wet and matted to his pale forehead with perspiration, was holding the weapon. He said to the other, "Joseph, we'd better alert government headquarters before we do any permanent damage to him. They will want to question him. He must be in good enough condition to answer their questions".

Joseph, his gray collarless uniform splattered with drops of Obadele's blood and his own sweat, was breathing heavily from his fierce and brutal exertion. He kicked Obadele's chest one more time, grunting and smiling when he heard the crack of a rib. His grinning face, bright red from his exertion loomed over Obadele as he bent over, holding his knees and said, "You're right, Barrington."

While Barrington aimed a laser handgun, set on destruct, at the unmoving form lying on the ground in a fetal position, Joseph pulled a videophone from his belt, punched in a code and awaited the reply. A man's face, with green eyes, a permanent scowl and short-cropped blonde hair appeared on the small screen, frowning. He growled, "What is it?"

Joseph, his bald head glistening with sweat from the exertion of beating Obadele, spoke softly, with obvious deference, "Commander, we discovered a Human trying to leave New Europa. He tried to resist us, but we subdued him."

Obadele was barely conscious but heard the exchange and would have smiled if he hadn't been in so much pain. Instead, he grimaced at the boldfaced lie. He had had weapons trained on him constantly after the guards forced him to undress and alternated beating him and holding the weapon on him. This barbaric violence had continued without pause for more than twenty minutes before Barrington thought to call their superior. They had such hate for him even though all they knew about him was that he was Human, representative of a group of people who had never done anything against them.

The Commander smiled wickedly, "Bring him to headquarters. I'll alert Joshua." After a pause, he demanded, "Let me see his face."

Joseph turned his body towards Obadele and yelled, "Sit up, Nag and uncover your face! I want to see it!" The word "nag" was a derogatory term for Human. No Horde remembered where it came from, but everybody had heard it used as long as they could remember.

Obadele fought the urge and instinct to lash out. Even in his battered condition, he felt that he could defeat them, but realized that he couldn't take the risk. He would have to wait until a better opportunity presented itself, so he obeyed the command and pulled himself up into a sitting position despite the pain in his chest. He hoped that his fractured ribs had not punctured his lungs. Obadele didn't feel short of breath, and it didn't hurt him to breathe deeply, so he felt confident that his lungs were intact.

When Joseph positioned the videophone in front of Obadele's face, the facial expression of the Commander on the screen changed from complacent irritation to shock. He quickly said, "Do not touch him again. Secure him well because he's very dangerous. Take him to Joshua's office immediately. I repeat, do no more damage to him and be very careful. Set your weapon on stun and not destruct. He must be taken to Joshua alive and in good condition. I am sending a squad to escort you into headquarters."

Joseph and Barrington clicked their heels together and saluted the Commander's image as the screen went dark. They looked at each other in amazement, and then they stared at Obadele.

Joseph asked Obadele, "Who are you, Nag? You must be very special. A whole squad just for you."

Obadele pretended to faint and did not answer.

The guards tied a magno-rope around Obadele's wrists, thighs and ankles and pinned his arms to his sides. They lifted him by his arms and carried him towards the copter parked several dozen yards up the street. When they passed an alley, two more blonde, blue-eyed men, dressed in similar uniforms, stepped behind them and touched their necks with stun rods.

Obadele started to fall as Joseph and Barrington fell and were unable to support his weight, but one of the second pair of guards caught him before he hit the ground. Obadele opened his eyes, his vision fuzzy as he tried to focus enough to see this second pair. He didn't know what to expect. One of the men spoke quickly, "We'll get you across the border before the escort arrives. The Commander obviously recognized you."

After releasing the magno-rope, the uniformed men gently guided Obadele as he staggered in pain, back to the alley from which they had come. "Can you make it into the alley by yourself?" the second man asked.

Obadele nodded and said, "Medasi Pi (Thank you very much)." Before he could finish the statement, the guards had vanished. He heard sirens in the distance and saw Joseph move slightly. Obadele stumbled into the alley. Three steps in, he heard a voice whisper, "Thank the Creator and the Blessed Ancestors. You made it".

Obadele felt four strong arms gently lift him into a copter, and he drifted off to sleep as the low hum signaled the take-off.

# CHAPTER ONE

## *The Horde Rises Again*

### <u>Amma</u>

Amma rushed to the window for what may have been the hundredth time and pressed her forehead to the glass, cupping her hands from her temples to the glass to reduce the glare. She thought she heard footsteps outside the door. Again, she peered out the narrow window hoping to see Obadele walking toward the front door. He wasn't there. She saw her image in the glass and barely recognized the face staring back at her. Her eyes were slightly bloodshot, and bags had formed under them. Her hair was unkempt, and her facial expression was vague. She smiled ironically and thought to herself, "So this is what sleep deprivation looks like." Dejected once again, Amma walked back into the room to continue her vigil.

She was frantic with worry about Obadele. He had always managed to keep in close contact with her when he was out scouting the Horde, but she had not spoken to or heard from him in seven days. Amma knew how mindlessly savage the Horde could be and shuddered whenever she thought of what might be happening to Obadele.

Amma was a beautiful woman, with dark brown dancing eyes framed by a heart-shaped face. Her facial expression was usually pleasant even when she wasn't smiling, which was rare. Her white teeth formed a perfect center for her dark chocolate complexion. Her short natural hair was usually perfect. This night, however, her eyes were flat, and the dance was no longer present in them.

She paced nervously through the darkened room and occasionally stopped to peer out of the window as if by looking, she could will him there, walking up to the door, back into her arms. The night was calm and very dark. Even after her eyes adapted to the darkness, she could see nothing. There were no sounds. She could not even hear insects. She especially missed hearing the crickets, and their absence made her feel even more alone.

Her thoughts drifted to the realities that she faced at age thirty-six. For thousands of years, life on planet Heart had been cyclical. Humanity had been forced to defend themselves from the Horde every century or two. There was even a 700 year period that had ended seven centuries previously, during which the Horde had actually prevailed and had gained control of Heart. The diabolically clever Horde leadership had almost destroyed Humanity and had brought the planet to near-complete destruction before Maat (truth, justice, righteousness, harmony, balance, order, and reciprocity) had finally prevailed. The Horde had actually rewritten and renamed TheStory. They called it "History." They had taken Human spiritual traditions and objectified them, thus transforming these hallowed traditions into meaningless, repetitive, materialistic, hypocritical, individualistic, superficial, and manipulatable rituals. They imposed this new structure, which they called "Religion," on Humanity.

Humans resisted at first, but the Horde concentrated their devious methods of brainwashing on the minds of Human children. After six generations, the Horde worldview was ingrained into the hearts and minds of Humanity. It became all that Humanity knew, and they assumed that it was their own and was universal. Many Humans were willing to fight and even die to defend the Horde and their Horde values. Actually, many did choose sides in Horde fraternal wars, being killed or maimed for "their" Horde, feeling that it was their duty.

There were some Humans, however, called Maroons, who refused to allow their culture and worldview to die. They met together, studied together, wrote and distributed books, articles, pamphlets, electronic communication, and holograms on TheStory and its importance to Humans. They also created music and art that conveyed these messages. They were political and cultural agitators and used all the available high tech communication methods to spread information about TheStory and the true culture of Humanity. The Horde ignored them initially because their numbers were small, and their means meager. The Maroons persisted, however, even though the information they valued so much was frequently rejected by their own people. But their numbers grew. When the Horde finally realized the seriousness of what was happening, they attempted to brutally suppress the Maroons, but it was too late. The more brutal the Horde became, the more Humans were converted back to their own TheStory. The Maroons had passed the desire for self-knowledge to their children, their families, and their communities. Indeed, each community still had shrines and places of honor for each of these Maroons that had influenced them until there were multiple generations of shrines.    Eventually, Humanity regained control of much of Heart.

Although the Horde leadership had projected fear of Human reprisal upon the Horde masses, it never materialized despite many opportunities. Because of the ethical fairness and spiritual nature of Humanity, many Horde were actually happy that Humans had regained control of Heart. These Horde individuals were called Loyalists, and many of them had even actively helped Humanity during the struggle.

Amma's favorite subject during her education and training had been "TheStory."  Indeed, she had done so well that she had become a professional StoryTeller and StoryUser. She had so excelled in her chosen field that she had been elevated to the prestigious and heavily responsible position of Paramount StoryTeller of New Alkebulan. Amma specialized in an era that fascinated and excited her but also filled her with great dread.  This was the seven hundred year period called The Maafa, the time of Great Disaster, when Humans were defeated by, enslaved by and subjected to the Horde.  The study of the Maafa was very difficult for Humans for several reasons. The Maafa took place over almost a millennium in the past, and there was great difficulty in recovering and correctly interpreting those records. Also, expertise in The Maafa required detailed understanding of the Horde as well as knowledge of Humanity during its lowest time. This memory was so powerful and so painful in most Humans that not many StoryTellers opted to study that time period. The term Maafa referred to the physical and spiritual violence and psychological damage suffered by Humanity at the hands of Horde during that disastrous period of TheStory. Amma's encyclopedic knowledge of that era of Human existence made her one of Heart's foremost experts on the Horde. That was how she had met Obadele.

Amma turned and looked at the large room, the room that she and Obadele had designed together. It was almost a perfect square, and the ceiling was 12 feet above the hardwood floor. The pale blue walls appeared bare except for murals of scenes of Humans in various activities. There were volumes of all kinds of books (old fashioned paper books, e-books, mini-CD books, holographic books and mini-DVD books) and music behind almost every square inch of the walls, neatly arranged in topical order. She walked to the center of the room where two chairs sat side by side, facing a screen that was three meters wide and almost took up the entire wall. The arms of the chairs were grooved so that a Human arm would fit comfortably in them. At the front of the arms, at the level of the hands, were several buttons. The buttons were the control center for all the functions of the room. Although one chair (her chair) was slightly smaller than the other, they were both sizable and pear-shaped and bent into a 110-degree angle.

She sat in the larger chair, Obadele's chair. The base extended upwards and adjusted automatically to her height. She pressed a button on the right arm of the chair, and soft, gentle, slow 6/8 drum rhythms filled the room, calming her spirit. Amma allowed the memories of the day she first saw him, almost ten years before, to wash over her. The chair continued to adjust to the contours of her slender, shapely frame, and she folded her legs under her body. She smelled his scent in the chair, and her pretty face melted into a smile. She never tired of thinking about Obadele.

When she and Obadele met as adults, she had just completed the requirements for the position of StoryTeller. She had been invited to participate in the Passage Ritual that officially inducted her into the life of a StoryTeller. Amma had actually been chosen by the teachers and her peers from the ten training classes located in centers all over New Alkebulan to give the main address. This great honor was the result of her hard work and discipline. The ceremony was held in Menefer, the largest city and capital of New Alkebulan. During the week-long festivities, she and the other StoryTeller candidates had met with prominent Elder StoryTellers. They addressed selected members of the Paramount Council of Elders of New Alkebulan, each speaking on a topic involving their areas of specialization.

On their way to the ceremony, walking out of Nkrumah Square, the huge pyramid-shaped hotel where they stayed, she again noticed a tall, slender, very handsome young man getting on the bus. He looked vaguely familiar. She had seen him the first day of their arrival, during the formal introductions. He was Kwame Omowale. Kwame was about 6'4" and had smooth ebony colored skin, full sensuous lips, short natural black hair and big brown luminous eyes. His eyelids arched in the center as if he was constantly analyzing everything around him. His posture was straight, and his expression confident. She remembered hearing her mother talking about the Omowales. Amma had even played with him and his siblings when they were very young, but she scarcely remembered, it had been so long ago. She had found out that Kwame was a StoryTeller candidate with a special focus on the Kemetic phase of Human development, a difficult era because it spanned more than ten millennia.

Assigned a seat near the front of the two-decker green oversized bus across the aisle from Kwame, Amma and several of the other young women slipped glances at him frequently as he was so good to look at. Kwame obviously enjoyed the attention of the beautiful young women because he would strike a pose whenever he felt their gazes on him. He had noticed Amma in particular and was struck by her beauty. He was shy, however, and continuously angry at himself for not striking up a conversation with her. Amma liked him, too. The way that she stared and smiled at him made it obvious. The pair had much in common, both being StoryTeller candidates. Because they had already been introduced formally at the initial reception, right after their arrival in Menefer, the official ice had been broken. Nothing stood in the way of him getting to know her except his shyness.

Amma hoped that she could get to know Kwame. She eventually wanted to marry, although she had given less thought to it than many women her age. She knew that the Elder Investigation before an engagement was allowed could take months. Kwame was so intelligent, so nice, and so very handsome; perhaps he was "the one".

The Elder Investigation was required by The Maatic Code that governed New Alkebulan. Before a couple could officially become engaged to be married, the Elders from both families wanted to be sure that the couple was compatible. This would confirm that the marriage would be a happy one, and any children born of that union would grow up in a stable and loving household, and grow up to be emotionally and psychologically healthy adults. Divorce was dreaded. It had been a major problem during the Maafa, so when the last Major Sep Tepi (or New Birth) of Humanity began, it was decided that all efforts to prevent the need for divorce would be made before marriage. They studied the previous seven generations of each person's lineage to ensure compatibility in all things, including and especially career choices, recreational interests, hobbies and motivation, as well as personality, spirituality, intelligence, physicality, and sexuality. Although time-consuming and sometimes disappointing, this custom worked very well.

Divorce was almost unheard of and there was very little evidence of incompatibility in any marriage. Disagreements naturally occurred occasionally, and arguments occurred even less frequently, but the Elders were so good at what they did that compatibility outweighed anything else. Almost all marriages were happy and content. Because of this, almost all couples adhered to the advice of the Elders, even though it wasn't dictated by law that they do so. If the Elders advised against marriage, they usually didn't marry, even if they felt that they loved each other deeply. They understood that love did not necessarily mean compatibility, but that compatibility almost always meant happiness for the couple and, more importantly, for their children. Amma knew from her studies that Human life had not always been so successful. During the Maafa, Humanity had high divorce rates as well as high domestic violence rates (child and spousal abuse), and unspeakable sexual looseness and deviancy. The spiritual aspect of sexuality, the sacred joining of male and female for completion, had been completely reduced to animalistic physical gratification, frequently anonymous.

The ground bus ride was very short. It seemed even shorter because Amma had been thinking of things other than the ride. The distance between the hotel and the Council

Chambers was only about 15 blocks. When the StoryTeller candidates arrived at the Council building, they exited the bus in a deliberate and orderly manner. They were guided directly to their seats in the Great Meeting Room of The Chamber, a room that would become very familiar to Amma.

When the candidates had been finally seated in the Paramount Council Chambers, she had experienced a moment that would change her life forever. While looking around the chamber, her eyes had met and locked into the most intense dark brown eyes that she had ever seen. They belonged to a very good looking young man who was standing in front of the podium. He looked to be slightly older than she and had a regal bearing. He resembled Kwame Omowale but did not have Kwame's striking good looks, although Amma also found him quite handsome. His complexion was not as dark as Kwame's, but his features were similar. He was bald, brown and fine (she remembered thinking about this term that she had learned from studying the Maafa). He was not as tall as Kwame. She guessed that he was about 5'11" tall, five inches taller than she was. He was also very powerfully built, although not extremely muscular. His facial expression seemed to betray a kind personality. Still, his piercing eyes suggested that he could rise to whatever level of gentleness or violence required by the situation in which he found himself.

Amma was fascinated with him. She noticed that he wore the purple kufi of a Protector and the white agbada of a Linguist. This fascinated her even more. As a Linguist, he was an expert in languages, communication, and diplomacy, and thus well educated. As a Protector, he was an expert in police tactics, military science, many styles of martial arts, intelligence gathering, and combat of all kinds. This was a very unusual combination. Linguists were highly educated, while Protectors usually had more training than formal education.

As she relived the memory of the first sight of the man she now loved so passionately, Amma hugged herself and rocked slowly and gently to and fro in his chair, smelling his scent, while the soft rhythms in the room continued to calm her restless spirit. She remembered that after they had seemingly been lost in each other's eyes for what seemed like an eternity, the sound of the drums signaling the entrance of the Council of Elders into the chamber broke the spell. The ceremony started, and the candidates gave their respective presentations. When her turn to speak came, she walked confidently to the podium. Although she was the focus of attention for everyone in the Great Hall, she only felt his eyes, feeling his gaze on her with every step. She did not lose her concentration and intensity, however, and went on to describe the differences in worldview and overall spiritual and cultural potential between Humanity and Horde. She was totally focused and lost herself in her presentation, and when she finished twenty minutes later, she received a thunderous standing ovation from everyone in the room.

At that point, she again became aware of the intense young man. This time he was smiling broadly with his face and eyes as he applauded her. She almost nodded imperceptibly to him reflexively before realizing, in horror, that she had almost initiated communication before formal introductions had been made. No one seemed to notice in the clamor, and at that moment, she made up her mind that she would meet him and find out all about him before they left Menefer that next evening.

She hadn't thought about Kwame on the way back to the hotel because her thoughts had been focused on the intense young man whose beautiful smile had almost made her break Maatic protocol. How would she make it right? When she found a dozen Black orchids at the doorway to her room without a card attached, she knew immediately who sent them. At first, she wondered how she would get back in touch with the sender without breaking protocol. Because they had not verbally spoken to each other or written a message, protocol had only been mildly bruised but not broken. In fact, if he had written a note, protocol dictated that they be formally introduced within minutes. Not only had they not been formally introduced, but she also didn't even know his name. She remembered, as a Protector, he was an expert in covert operations. Amma then realized that he would overcome all obstacles and find her. She had a warm feeling of contentment and safety, a feeling she had only felt before in her father's arms, yet this was different.

Later that evening, at the Karamu (Feast) of Celebration, a note under her glass said, "Please, smile if we should talk." She knew at once that the note was from him and smiled her prettiest smile as she immediately looked up and around the large room (she could not have stopped the smile even if she had tried). Almost immediately, she saw the intense young man walking across the room towards her, accompanied by Kwame, of all people. Kwame did not look very happy but dutifully introduced Obadele to Amma. She learned that they were brothers, sons not of the same woman or even of two sisters, but sons of identical twin sisters and identical twin brothers. Since that initial introduction, she had frequently teased Obadele by asking how he knew she would smile and get him off the hook of a major protocol violation. He never answered but gave her that whimsical smile that always melted her.

When she spoke with her mother, Nzinga, that night and excitedly told her about the Omowales, she was surprised that her mother knew them so well. Nzinga reminded Amma that she had played together with Kwame, Obadele, and their sister, Aisha when they were all small children. Amma had no specific memories of those playtimes, and her mother told her that they had not seen each other in many years since then.

After Kwame had formally introduced them, he had gracefully excused himself. Amma would never forget Obadele's first words to her. He had looked deeply into her eyes and said earnestly, "The brilliance of your mind and the enormity of your beauty are exceeded only by the purity of your spirit, Amma. Yet, it is your smile that blows me away."

That did it!! Some of her friends would call him corny or sappy, but for the first time in her life, she was truly and deeply in love. She had always concentrated more on her studies and her career goals than she had concentrated on men. However, she had just been given a different focus that would change her life forever.

The loud ring-buzz of the videophone jerked her back to reality. She anxiously pressed the Black "receive" button without looking to see who was calling, and, to her immense relief, the ruggedly handsome features of her husband filled the wall screen in front of her. His eyes, as intense as ever, were framed by his oval-shaped face, nut-brown complexion and generous lips. She saw that he had a worried expression. Reading her look of concern, he quickly said, "I'm safe, baby."

She immediately felt tons lighter and his words swept away the heavy burdens that his facial expression had initially placed on her. She exhaled deeply and audibly and said, almost in a whisper, "Thank the Ancestors!!! I was so worried! Are you sure you're all right? Where are you? How long have you been back? Why haven't you called me sooner? When can I see you?" Her words seemed to pay homage only to her emotions as they seemed to leave her mouth without originating in her brain.

He looked away for a fleeting moment as if he was searching for the right words. He looked directly into her eyes and said, "I was captured by the Horde for a few minutes, but Loyalists helped me to escape almost immediately. I got away before they could really hurt me, thanks to our Loyalist friends. I've been in Menefer for only about an hour." He ended by gently saying, "I'm really okay, sweetheart."

As his words sank in, her soft features froze into a mask of terror. She knew what unspeakable horrors that Horde prisoners were subjected to. In fact, only those who had experienced it knew more of what Horde prisoners were imperiled to than she did. The fact that her husband had been a prisoner horrified her. She knew that even if he had escaped major torture, he had been beaten terribly. She carefully and intently examined the face on the screen, looking for bruises and scars.

He seemed to read her mind again and said, "They didn't do anything to seriously hurt me. They recognized me almost immediately and were planning the major interrogation. They didn't want to do anything to risk hurting me before trying to extract information from me. Joshua himself was to have interrogated me."

She shuddered.

Obadele was Chief Protector of the Paramount Council of Elders and was a member of the Expanded Council of Governance in New Alkebulan. He was truly a prize catch for the Horde because of the strategic information that he was exposed to. It was no wonder that Joshua, the Horde leader, had planned to personally interrogate him.

Joshua was a sadistic leader who was well known for his brutal and ruthless tactics in achieving his goals during interrogations. Amma loved Obadele more than she loved her own life. She would have gladly suffered any torture and would die for him and knew that he felt the same way about her. She was frustrated that he personally went on these dangerous missions, but understood that he was the best person to perform those tasks.

They were both anxiously awaiting the magical tenth anniversary of their marriage because they would finally be allowed to start their family. The Maatic Code prohibited couples whose youngest partner had married between twenty-five and thirty years of age to have children before the tenth wedding anniversary. This was called the Welsing Doctrine and ensured that children would be born to mature parents who were sure of their relationship, knew each other well, and who agreed on the important aspects of childrearing. Amma remembered that her grandparents had bitterly resented this rule all their lives. It had been initiated shortly before they were married. However, the average life expectancy at that time was only ninety-five years. The life expectancy had currently improved to an average of 128 years, and it was not unusual to hear of people living useful lives at the age of 160 years. Interestingly, the average age at the start of menopause had increased to eighty years, although the average family size of six had not changed.

The Maatic Code also stated that no one should marry before the age of twenty-five years, and age differences of more than ten years were severely frowned upon. If the youngest partner was between thirty and thirty-five years old, the couple waited five years before having children. If the youngest partner was thirty-six or older, at least two years had to elapse before a family was started. Amma and Obadele had married three months before her twenty-fifth birthday because of considerations in both their educational processes.

As Amma carefully studied the familiar image of her beloved husband, she realized that something was wrong! He wasn't telling her everything! She started to speak, but he again anticipated her question and said, "The Horde is preparing for another offensive, soon."

Her heart sank, and she briefly forgot her immediate concern for him. She could only ask, "So soon?" But her mind raced. Humanity had not completely recovered from the last Horde offensive. The toll in Human and Horde life and suffering during these offensives was always staggering. It seemed so useless. She couldn't understand why most of the Horde were unable to live in any society, no matter how peaceful or how just, that was not only not created by them but not controlled by them. It almost seemed as if they were incapable of contributing to and assimilating into a culture they did not create or control. At the same time, they demanded that Humanity live within the Horde's own chaotic system.

The Horde had ideas about freedom and progress that seemed very strange to Humans. They valued individual freedom above group cooperation, and they viewed progress as the increased ability to more efficiently control and destroy whatever they wanted to control and destroy. Although they spoke highly of family values, their actions did not support their words. Many of the men married men and women married women. Older men and women molested young boys and girls. Promiscuity and infidelity were rampant, men and women abandoned their partners, spousal and child abuse occurred frequently, and their divorce rate was more than 90% in both heterosexual and homosexual marriages. Violence was endemic, and violence, especially fighting, was considered to be the highest form of entertainment. Hunting and killing animals not needed for food was another wildly popular form of entertainment. It was even rumored that some Horde "hunting clubs" kidnapped Humans to have "exciting" hunting experiences. Even if this was not true, many of the most popular Horde films had some variation of this theme in their plots.

As might be expected, Horde population numbers were dwindling steadily. Although they had a steadily decreasing birth rate, they did not seem to want to survive. They were the ultimate suicidal group that would not be satisfied until they had destroyed everything else along with themselves. Despite their strange ideas about the absolute supremacy of the individual, they exhibited shared group insanity and "herd instinct" (hence the name, "Horde"). This insanity seemed to be pulling them towards a violent oblivion and extinction, and they wanted Humanity to share this fate.

Sometimes Amma wanted to seal them off and let them destroy themselves. She knew that if left alone without the stabilizing influence of Humanity, the Horde would rapidly disappear and possibly become extinct. With her knowledge of TheStory, she realized that Humans had profoundly affected every era of Horde HisStory for the better. Ironically, Humans had served as the Horde conscience, even during the Maafa. The Horde also knew this, but instead of stabilizing their societies with Maat, they concentrated their political and "moral-religious" efforts on imposing rules on every aspect of life, for absolute control of even minute and mundane details. Their scientific and technological efforts were used in cloning and attempting to create life, an homage to their "god-complex." They also exerted much of their genius in creating even more effective, efficient, and devastating weapons of mass destruction.

Amma always scolded herself for thinking those thoughts because she knew that it would not be Maatic to intentionally allow them to destroy themselves. She also knew, as a practical consideration, that the Horde would not allow themselves to be sealed off. As sure as moths are attracted to light, the Horde had to attack Humanity periodically. She again reflected on the fact that the attack was coming at a much sooner interval than usual.

She drew in a quick breath and jerked her head to the side and started to comment, but before she could say anything, Obadele quickly said, "I'll still be in Menefer tonight. You should meet me at "The Spot" in "Our Place" as soon as you can get here."

She found herself smiling despite all the bad news she was getting. Beginning with the period of seclusion after their marriage, they had always stayed in the Diop penthouse suite at the pyramid shaped hotel, Nkrumah Square, during their frequent visits to Menefer. Since then, they had always called the hotel "The Spot" and the suite "Our Place." Obadele was not smiling, however.

He continued, "I've contacted the Paramount Council and asked Jomo to meet with us tonight. There's no time to lose."

Her smile disappeared as her brow once again furrowed into a worried look. She replied, "I'll see you in no more than three hours. "

He smiled nervously and said, "I love, respect, and see you."

She melted completely. That nervous smile of his had more power over her than the worst that the Horde could do. She replied, glowingly, "Love and respect to you also, my Love. I do see you."

As the screen went dark, she immediately replayed their conversation in her mind. He was worried and that made her worry. The Horde, while still immature and juvenile in their development as a people and capable of terribly barbaric and destructive "tantrums," were technological geniuses. Because of their biological inability to experience anything of a truly spiritual nature and their developmental lack of empathy, they filled their spiritual void constantly by attempting to master the material universe through intellectual effort alone. They also acted out wide ranges of behavior to experience emotions based on maximal adrenalin stimulation. Otherwise, they couldn't feel anything. Much of their forms of entertainment focused on exhibiting terrifying images and ghoulish fantasies.

Many of them even loved inflicting as well as experiencing pain. Because they had become so adept at these behaviors, they were, indeed, formidable enemies.

Amma had a horrible thought. What if the Horde had done some psychobiological tampering with Obadele's brain or his psyche? What if they had implanted devices into his body for monitoring, or worse? She trembled with her next thought ... suppose they had implanted explosives into his body timed to explode when he was in the Paramount Council chambers. They knew that he had to report his findings to the Council. As much as she loved him, she knew that both their primary obligations were to Humanity and not to each other. She realized that he had already thought of all the things that were now causing her skin to crawl and her scalp to itch. He would have de-toxified and cleansed himself before calling her (unless he was placed under the mind and body control of Horde technology). She was supremely confident that he would never knowingly endanger Humanity or her.

She keyed in Kwame's code on the videophone almost frantically. Since her marriage to Obadele, she and Kwame had become very close. In fact, she had introduced Kwame to his wife, Aset, her best friend. After four ring buzzes, Aset's image appeared on the wall screen where Obadele's image had just been.

"Hotep (Peace) Amma! Wo ho te sane (How are you?), Sister?" Aset said with a broad smile. She was obviously genuinely happy to greet Amma.

It had always been like that with Amma and Aset. They had been girls together in New Atlantis, in the up-south region of New Alkebulan and had been in the same age-grade during the community Rites of Passage. They were actually born on the same day in the same birthing place, and it seemed as if they had been together since their birth. They were so close that in school, they were called "Double A". Even if for some reason, they did not communicate for months (which was rare), when they finally got together, the interval of their separation seemed like only minutes.

Aset immediately sensed that something was not right with her friend. "What's wrong, Amma," she asked.

"I'm worried about Obadele," Amma said flatly.

"Haven't you heard from him yet," Aset asked, with a concerned expression and tone.

"Yes, I just spoke with him," Amma admitted, "but I just know that something is wrong. I'm going to meet him in New Menefer tonight, and I'd like you and Kwame to go with me. I don't want to say too much now, but I'll explain as much as I can on the way."

Seeing the worried look on her friend's face, Aset agreed immediately. Even though she and Kwame had made plans for that night, she knew that Kwame would agree. He adored Amma, and Obadele was more than Kwame's "big brother," he was Kwame's idol. Amma was not a worrier, so Aset did not take her worried expression lightly.

Aset, in her best take-charge manner, said, "We'll take our copter. You don't look like you need to be driving. How long do you think we'll be in New Menefer?"

"Hopefully, no more than two or three days. A week at the most," Amma answered gratefully. She really didn't feel like driving or traveling alone.

Kwame's face joined his wife's on the screen. He had probably been in the room from the start of the conversation. Amma hoped that she hadn't interrupted them during one of the lovemaking sessions they were so famous for in family circles. Their relationship was extremely passionate, and they loved making love more than most couples. They had the videophone screen settings adjusted to head only, so Amma guessed that they were probably nude. From their perspective, the Elders had been exactly right in allowing their union.

Kwame said, "Hotep, Amma."

She returned his greeting but reflected silently that there would probably be no peace for a while.

"We'll throw some things into a bag and pick you up in about thirty minutes. I'll call Aisha and let her know that Obadele is alright."

If Amma was worried about Obadele, then Kwame was also.

## Kwame

Kwame felt a growing, dull, gut-wrenching panic but tried to look calm for his wife's benefit. Amma was obviously worried about Obadele, and this frightened him. She was always cool, calm, and level headed and not easily frightened. If she was worried, something must be very wrong. He and Aset looked at each other without speaking for what seemed like hours, even though it was only a few seconds. Words were not necessary.

They got up from their super king-sized circular bed that was located in a large circular room with the bed's head barely touching the purple wall, directly across from the bathroom. The walls were not completely bare, having multiple paintings and old fashioned photographs of Humans in various poses placed around the room. They quickly showered together, dressed and packed a large bag for the two of them.

Aset was a voluptuous brown woman with a shaved head and bright eyes. She wore a sleek one-piece oversized gown in red based kente print. Even though it completely covered her, it clung to her curves in such a way that made Kwame stare and swallow hard. Kwame wore simple black matching pants and a three-quarter length sleeved shirt they called a government suit. It took them about ten minutes to get to Amma and Obadele's home, traveling in the second level in their copter. The copter was beige with dark brown trimmings shaped like the body of a wingless twenty-first-century jet plane and about as long as two twenty-first century SUVs and almost twice as wide. The blades were internal, and the engines ran silently. Their copter could comfortably seat up to twelve adults. It used a plant fuel that was common in the environment. It could be grown in the fields or manufactured inexpensively, even in a home lab without risk of explosion or toxicity. Despite the size of the copter, it only required refueling about every six months.

There were three levels of travel in New Alkebulan. The ground level permitted low speeds and pedestrians, as well as ground-based vehicles like cars, trucks, buses, motorcycles, bicycles, and the like. The top speed on the ground level was 75 miles per hour. The second level was designed for hovercraft and some copters. It extended well above the city skylines (of which there were few since people preferred to live in communities that were spread out rather than stacked on top of each other). The maximum speed on the second level was 150 miles per hour. The top-level was reserved only for programmable copters. Each copter entering the third level was programmed for a speed of 150 to 225 miles per hour.

Amma was ready when they arrived. She heard the copter set down on the helipad in the yard and walked out of the house. Amma smiled when she was close enough to see their faces in the darkness. Kwame had gotten out of the copter to open the baggage compartment and waited outside to take her bags. She had two bags since she had packed some things for Obadele. Amma was also not sure that he'd be returning to Abydos with her but was determined not to leave his side.

Kwame programmed a course on the autopilot in the copter so that he could ride in the back with the ladies. It was good that it was so late because autopilot could only be used when the upper-level traffic density was very low. Although the autopilot caused the copter to move at slower average speeds of about 175 miles per hour, it was very convenient. It would take about ninety minutes to get to Menefer from their home in midtown Abydos. Kwame watched the street shrink, and the rows of single-family houses and duplexes gradually disappear. He observed the two ladies in talk. They were so animated when they were together. It was obvious that they deeply loved and knew each other well. They finished each other's thoughts as if they were twins communicating telepathically, almost like his mothers.

Amma's short, naturally curly Black hair was beginning to show small streaks of premature gray. It looked good on her. Kwame had known Amma for twelve years, and she was still as beautiful as she was when he first noticed the lithe, beautiful, and intense young woman. He wanted to court her himself but had been intimidated by her single-minded intensity at learning all that she could about the Maafa. In retrospect, he realized that they were not meant to be together as mates. She was, however, a perfect match for Obadele, whom he had called "O" since they were children. Amma and O matched each other in so many ways, especially in the intensity in which they dedicated themselves to Humanity. Nana Ade, Kwame, Aisha and Obadele's beloved maternal grandfather, had helped him to realize that Amma was not only more suited to be O's wife but that she was also a perfect friend for him.

As he watched the ladies talk energetically, his mind wandered back to the night, almost ten years previously at the Karamu of Celebration following his and Amma's presentations to the Council. He had actually been trying to overcome his shyness and think of ways to strike up a conversation with Amma when O asked him to formally introduce him to her. He had been disappointed because he realized at that point that whatever chance he may have had with Amma was gone. O had not even asked any questions about her, which was unusual for anyone with a security background. He just wanted to break the official ice so that he could converse with her. Refusing O was not even a consideration. O was his big brother, the son of his mother's twin sister, his other mother and the son of his father's twin brother, his other father. Although there was a five-year difference in their ages and O was in the next older age-grade, they were extremely close. O had taught him how to protect himself, had encouraged him to be a top scholar and had demonstrated, by example, the pursuit of excellence that Nana Ade had taught them all.

Nana Ade had assured him that the Elders would most probably not have certified a marriage between him and Amma. He now felt very thankful as he looked at his wife with an inward smile. Aset was taller than Amma, almost as tall as he was. She had high cheekbones, and her complexion was smooth ebony. She was voluptuous with a narrow waist, beautifully rounded buttocks and firm grapefruit-sized breasts. Her head was shaven bald. She must have felt his gaze on her because she looked up at him and smiled. Her smile created a dull delicious ache in his heart and his loins. He loved her powerfully in so many ways and on so many levels. Their conversations were frequently as stimulating as their lovemaking.

He was grateful to Amma for introducing him to Aset at the Central Ceremony during her and O's Wedding Week. He knew that Amma had hoped that he and Aset would like each other, and they did not disappoint her. He was O's First Attendant at the wedding, and Aset was Amma's First Attendant, so they were officially paired. He had been fascinated by the tall, bubbly, witty, voluptuous, energetic, brilliant, and beautiful young woman that he found himself paired with during the week-long festivities. After the first ceremony, the formal introductions of the wedding party, they were hopelessly in love.

On the surface, their career choices could not have been more different. Kwame was a StoryTeller and Aset was a Healer. The fact was, however, that his specialty dealt with the cultural and, ultimately, spiritual health of the whole society and hers dealt with the physical and mental health of the individual people in the society.

As the ladies chatted, he let his mind go back to their wedding ceremony. He and Aset had worn identical purple and gold outfits -his, an agboda, and hers, an asoki. His mother, Adwoa and O's mother, Agya had been so happy. They smiled continuously during every minute of every day during that week. They had even smiled in their sleep. Kwame was so delighted to see those smiles because neither of them had smiled for a long time.

Nana Ade, in his role as Presiding Elder and Representative of the Ancestors, had poured libation for his and O's fathers, Osei and Opuku Buah. Osei and Opuku had been killed during a Horde uprising when Kwame was very young, so he had no direct memory of either of them. He had only been about two years old when Osei was killed, but he knew all about his father. He had photographs, videos and holograms of his father that were taken before Osei's transition to the Ancestral world. Kwame had even done many research projects on aspects of his father's life as an integral part of his studies. He remained in close spiritual communion with his father and poured libation for him daily at the Ancestral shrine in his home.

O remembered their fathers better because he had been older. Both Osei and Opuku were Scholar-Warriors. Their expertise made them dangerous to the Horde. Their first-hand knowledge of Joshua, with whom they had grown up, made them even more dangerous. In fact, Joshua, the primary Horde leader, had made special arrangements for them to be killed.

Nana Ade had fulfilled the roles of both father and grandfather to Obadele, Kwame and Aisha, their sister, and they missed him very much. Ade had made his transition to the Ancestral Realm less than one year earlier. Ade had been one hundred sixty-eight years old, although, as his body lay in state during the month-long funeral, he looked as he had when he was fifty years old.

Nana had served as Chief of the Paramount Council of Elders for many peaceful years before the Horde uprising killed his two sons-in-law. He retired in order to help his daughters recover from the horrible trauma that had been inflicted on them and to assist in the rearing of his grandchildren. Because of his experience and wisdom, however, he remained available for consultation with his successor and protege, Jomo Ajani. Amma's mother, Nzinga, had also been his protege but had declined being considered for the position. Her husband and son had been killed, and she wanted to concentrate on rearing Amma.

Kwame's thoughts turned to his sister, Aisha. Although she was very pleased with her older brother's choice of a wife, during the marriage festivities, she had been more anxious than anyone else in the family, including the bride and groom. Her nervous energy caused her to constantly move all over the Banquet building, ensuring everything was exactly right. She was Amma's Second Attendant and took her responsibilities very seriously (he had teased her that she took everyone else's responsibilities as seriously as she had taken her own).

Kwame loved his sister dearly. Aisha was tall, about the same height as Aset and had a light brown, mocha complexion and long, wavy Black hair. Although her features were sharp, she was extremely attractive. She was very bright but also very vulnerable. When they were children, Kwame always felt that he needed to protect her, even though she had excelled in their martial arts training and often defeated him.

Kwame and Aisha did not share the same biological father. Before killing Osei and Opuku, Joshua had forced them to watch him rape Adwoa. He had planned to do the same with Agya, but Ade and the Human military forces had discovered his hiding place before he could complete his plan. He quickly decapitated the husbands as their wives watched in horror before he made his escape. He had hoped to impregnate both of Ade's daughters and introduce Horde blood into the Omowale family, one of the most respected leadership clans of Humanity.

After the rape and murders, Adwoa and Agya became withdrawn. Neither of them spoke a word to anyone for months, and neither smiled for years. Adwoa's rape and the witnessing of their husbands' brutal murders weighed heavily on them. When Adwoa had discovered that she was pregnant, she had begged the Creator to make sure that Osei was the father. She had refused diagnostic methods of determining the identity of the father, but when Aisha was born, she knew that Joshua was the father. She had been offered the opportunity to terminate the pregnancy but refused.

Only pregnancies resulting from Horde rapes could be legally terminated. She chose to give birth to the child, however, and to keep it (as most women did). Abortion held a negative stigma for those women who had undergone one, even if they had conceived as the result of a rape. They were considered "destroyers of life." Although rape was virtually unheard of among Humans, it was still a major problem among the Horde, and there were always dozens of rapes during Horde uprisings. Their sexual confusion and deviancy were visited upon any Human women, girls, and boys they encountered. They also even raped Loyalist women during these times.

Because of the profound Human belief in the sanctity of life and the spirituality of the conceptual act between men and women, the prohibition of homosexuality was one of the few aspects of the Maatic Code whose violation evoked a visceral and frequently physically violent response. Human boys who were raped (and their fathers) usually became the fiercest warriors and frequently had to be observed carefully during battle to keep them from lapsing into Horde-like savage violence.

Adwoa had been honest with Kwame, Aisha, and O about everything, including Aisha's conception. Although she realized that she was a Mulat, half-Human and half-Horde, Aisha never felt unloved and never doubted her place in the Omowale family. She chose to honor Osei as her Father-Ancestor. She knew from all that she had read or heard about Osei from other family members that the bond between him and Adwoa was so strong that if he had survived, he would have loved and accepted Aisha and raised her as his own. She felt that he had been more of a father, even as an Ancestor, than Joshua could have ever been. The example of excellence that Osei left meant more to her than Joshua's evil and cruel genius. Hence, she loved, honored, and protected Osei's memory even more aggressively than did her brother, even though she had never known him.

Aisha had become a Linguist-Communicator. She was among the first women to choose that area as their specialty. She loved to talk and had a knack for languages. She had also excelled in political science, diplomacy and public speaking. Centuries previously, Humanity had realized that there were important cultural concepts inherent in every language that became lost in translation. Using the Diopian-Thiong'o Language Hypothesis, these concepts were captured intentionally in one language, a hybrid language that had become the main language of Heart. It was called Twish. Even the Horde spoke it although many of the concepts, especially those referring to spiritual and empathic matters, were alien to them and had been given new, superficial meanings by them. Many of the languages that comprised Twish were hybrids themselves. The main component languages of Twish were Twi, Mdw Ntr, Ki-Swahili, English, Yoruba, Ewe, Hausa, French, Xhosa, Zulu, and Spanish.

Kwame was very proud of Aisha. She had developed into a mature, brilliant, and beautiful young woman. Her only problem was that she seemed to have a penchant for becoming romantically interested in men who were wrong for her. The Elders had rejected four of her proposed engagements already, and she had been crushed each time. This was the only area of her life, where her confidence was not supreme. She had experienced bouts of depression during which she cursed her Horde blood for what she called, "making her unfit for a Human man." She had even transiently considered taking a Horde mate, chosen from among the Loyalists. She was aesthetically repulsed by them, however, and those thoughts were very brief.

The soft hum of the engine as the copter made a turn brought Kwame back to an acute awareness of his surroundings. Amma and Aset were quietly staring at him and smiling impishly. Aset asked, "Where were you, my love?"

"I was just reliving our marriage week," Kwame replied and quickly added, "We need to contact Aisha so that she'll know what's going on." He looked at his brother's wife and asked, "What is going on Amma?"

Amma smiled mischievously, "You really have not been here. That's what we've been discussing for the past thirty minutes". She solemnly added, "Obadele was captured by the Horde and found out that they are planning another offensive. He said that he was OK and that some undercover Loyalists helped him to escape, but he looked odd as if there was something else going on."

"I was asking Aset," Amma continued, "whether there was a technology in which controlling, monitoring, or explosive devices could be implanted into a Human body without being detected?"

"Is there?" Kwame looked at his wife.

"I'm not aware of it, if it exists," Aset stated as she wrinkled her brow. "Although those devices can be implanted, they should show up on routine scanning and imaging studies, and I'm sure the Council does that for anyone who returns from a mission behind enemy lines."

"You never can tell with the Horde," Kwame heard himself say in a horrified voice that, even to him, seemed to originate outside of his body. "They believe that 'progress' is creating new technology, regardless of its negative effect on themselves or their environment."

The three of them lapsed into a tense silence, hoping and praying that Kwame was wrong, but knowing that he could very well be right.

## Aset

Kwame had not wanted Aset to answer the videophone that night, but she felt compelled to answer, especially when she saw that Amma was calling. She had been feeling that something was wrong and was glad that she had answered. She had rarely seen Amma as worried as she appeared when her image appeared on the screen. It was shocking to Aset and to Kwame to see Amma that way. She was usually very poised, supremely confident, and infectiously happy. However, after hearing what Amma had to say, she was worried also. Although Amma was her age grade sister and lifelong best friend, her concern went deeper because she was also very worried about O. While she had married into the Omowale clan, they were all as close to her as her own blood. O had personally welcomed her into the family and had been kind and gracious to her, so although she adored her husband, she loved his brother and sister deeply, as well. It seemed as if they had always been together. They had become like parts of her own body. She really felt complete when she was with them. She was prepared to do anything to make sure that her loved ones remained safe.

Her own family had been decimated by the Horde. Indeed, everyone she knew had been negatively affected to some extent by the Horde. Because of this, she was sometimes disappointed that the Elders taught the people not to hate or be bitter. Hatred and bitterness could be so immediately satisfying. However, as a Healer, she understood that strong negative emotions like hate, fear, bitterness, and jealousy speeded up the deterioration of the physical and spiritual health of Humans. She also knew that these negative emotions retarded the return of Wholeness, which Humanity had lost ages previously, because of the Horde. She also knew that powerful negative feelings could impede the attainment of Wholeness across generations.

During the Pre-Kemetic Era of TheStory, Humans had been able to communicate with each other telepathically. They had also been able to communicate with many of their immediate Ancestors as well as with beings in the spirit world and in parallel dimensions. Many Humans had been able to fly, and most could levitate objects. When the Horde arose the first time, Humanity was suddenly forced to fight to save their civilization, and indeed, save Heart from being destroyed. This fighting, and the emotions required to fight, effectively weakened and destroyed the Wholeness of many Humans. With each Horde uprising after that first time, increasing numbers of Humans lost Wholeness. After the Maafa, no Human was Whole. The re-attainment of Wholeness was the goal of all Healers and Wholy Persons. Now that Humanity had reached a milestone level of Wholeness, they knew that they could use Wholeness to protect themselves without imposing any negative or destructive actions on the Horde. They just hadn't reached that level of knowledge/ development and the Horde was determined to destroy or subjugate Humanity before that process was completed.

Aset had become a Healer because she had felt stirrings in her head that she was certain were vestiges of Wholeness. She wanted to be a significant participant in Humanity's attempts to become Whole again. She also became a Healer because of the positive influence of Nzinga Asantewa, Amma's mother. When her family was killed, Nzinga took her in and completed her education and became a mother to her.

Aset's specialty was in the NeuroMental system. She had helped with Amma's original research, which dealt with the comparative worldview of Humanity and Horde, especially as it related to the Maafa. She was extremely gratified that Amma had acknowledged her contributions verbally, during her presentation to the Council as well as in the printed document, as was more common. Thus, knowledge of her research became more widely known, and people with helpful knowledge and experiences contacted her, often with extremely helpful information. There was no hesitation for this type of cooperativeness. It was well known that every contribution would be acknowledged, even though few Humans actually sought credit for their work in support of Humanity.

She had continued the comparative research on the pineal gland in Human and Horde that had begun during the late Maafa by legendary and honored scholars such as Richard King and Carol Barnes. She found that the pineal functioned at about 85-95% effectiveness in Humans and functioned at no more than 25% effectiveness, if at all, in most Horde. This finding, although deemed nonsignificant by Horde scientists, marked the beginning of the branch of science called "Duality" studies, of which Aset and Amma were celebrated as being the founders.

Aset and Amma's work led to the recognition that there was a relationship, which must be balanced, between mental/intellectual functioning and spiritual awareness. This relationship was optimized with good physical conditioning. Comparisons between Axiology, symbolic imagery, ontology, cosmology, and epistemology and other areas had been done almost a millennium earlier. Still, Aset and Amma had quantitated the differences based on precise measurement of pineal function. This had heralded a new era of Human-Horde relations.

They were able to show definitively that Human and Horde were essentially the same except for superficial differences in appearance and significant differences in spiritual/empathic potential. This difference profoundly altered the Horde ability to get along with others. This inability to get along with others had been called "psychopathic" by many Human pioneer Healers (The Wright Theorem). The documentation of this fact enabled human healers who specialized in Kmistry to create replacement Pineal hormones and enzymes called Pex (short for Pineal Extract). With Pex, Horde could become spiritually Human-like and actually become empathic. Many chose to do so and lived useful and peaceful lives, fully integrated into Human society. These Horde, called Loyalists, monitored their dosages carefully because overdoses caused a dissociative madness frequently followed by an extremely painful death. Pex was manufactured and provided to the Loyalists as needed without the need for payment or reciprocity.

Aset's trusted assistant, Jay, was a Loyalist. He had been a minor celebrity earlier in his life after having been found to have the highest natural pineal function ever found in Horde. As a child, he had been much more quiet and peaceful and had not displayed much of the hyperactivity and almost slapstick violence commonly seen in Horde children. This fact brought him to the attention of local peace monitors who suggested that he be tested. His findings stimulated the start of routine testing of all Horde and Human newborns. For replacement, he only required a very small dose of Pineal

Extract (Pex). He was, in fact, almost Human. When he decided on a career in Healing, there was no doubt in his mind that he wanted to work with Aset Wusu-Omowale. She was the acknowledged expert in his area of interest (pineal function), and he felt that he could not only learn a lot from her but could also be of great help to her as a type of living experiment. His high level of natural integrity made him willing to make great personal sacrifices to improve Heart.

Aset liked him very much, and because she respected his work and his integrity, she depended on him greatly. She had previously felt sorry for him. Even without replacement, he could have never fit in with the Horde, even though he looked like them with his tall stature, blonde hair, pink skin and bright blue eyes. His demeanor was too gentle and his outlook too peaceful for him to survive among his own people, and he was fully aware of this fact.

Jay was the subject of a private study that he and Aset were conducting, with the consent of the Council. It had previously been believed that only Humans could achieve Wholeness, but it was theorized that if Horde could reach Wholeness, perhaps they might become Human. There was at least one other factor besides pineal function that enabled Humans to tolerate the high levels of pineal activity believed present in the state of Wholeness. They had not yet been able to identify that factor. At those high levels of pineal activity, Humans reached a higher level of function but not to the level of complete Wholeness. At high levels of pineal activity, but significantly below those of Wholeness in Humans, Horde went mad and died. The goal of Aset and Jay's private study was to discover the additional factor or factors (called the Aha Factor), synthesize or isolate them, and give them to Jay. Their reasoning was that if any Horde could achieve Wholeness, it would be Jay.

Aset thought it ironic that Humans had been trying for millennia to peacefully coexist with Horde, despite the obvious fear, hatred and jealousy that Horde displayed in their repeated acts of horrific violence towards Humanity. Humans were always the bearers of the olive branch of peace, no matter what had been done to them. Kwame often spoke to her about how his grandfather, Ade, had fought so bravely, honorably and successfully against the Horde so many times, but was always willing to be the first to offer peace.

Jay had married Mae, a young woman who, like Aisha, was Mulat. Her parents were married, however, and she was not the product of a Horde rape as was Aisha. Her mother was descended from several generations of Loyalists. Aset frequently teased them about their rhyming names. Aset was fascinated with the prospect of them having children. Jay and Mae had offered to periodically test their children, but Aset only wanted to see the initial studies and did not want to subject them to that type of study as an ongoing process.

Most Horde refused the Pineal Replacement Therapy, however, and lived lives full of violence, brutality, hypocrisy, and hedonism. They were insulted that Humans saw them as being almost Human with several deficiencies.

Aset made a mental note to contact Jay early the following morning so that he'd know not to expect her in the lab for a few days. She had no worries about the work of her lab continuing effectively. Jay was a gifted administrator as well as a Healer and would be able to carry on without her. With. this comforting thought, she subsequently dozed off to sleep.

## Obadele

After hanging up the phone, Obadele slumped to his knees because of the severe pain that he felt. It had been difficult for him to deceive Amma, and it had drained him both physically and emotionally to do it. He had never lied to her, but he couldn't bear the thought of her anguish if she knew how badly he had been beaten, so he felt it necessary to minimize his injuries. As a StoryTeller, she knew how Humans captured by Horde were beaten and tortured, and he needed for her to remain as calm and objective as possible. The next few months would be critical to Humanity, and her dispassionate expertise would be sorely needed. He felt that they were reaching the stage of Meggidio, The Final Confrontation and that the future of Humanity, indeed of Heart, was at stake.

Meggidio was an ancient term that he had learned from Kwame. During the last eras of Kmt, one of the earliest recorded Human civilizations, a confederation of proto-Horde, called the Sea Peoples, had made several all-out attacks on Humanity. The final battle, won by Humanity, took place on the plains of a place called Meggidio. This was later known as Armageddon by Humans during the period of Horde dominance called the Maafa. During that time, the word "Meggidio" became the symbol of the mythical final battle between good and evil that was to happen in the future.

Based on what little Obadele had been able to find out before his capture, it appeared that Joshua had unified the various Horde factions under his leadership. He was preparing for an all-out attack on Humanity, using several new weapons that they had developed. The Loyalists who remained in Horde territory were extremely worried that this plan might actually succeed. The information about the weapons was a very tightly guarded secret, and he had been unable to get any details about the type of weapons created.

While in Neuveau Berlin, the capital city of Europa, the Horde homeland, Obadele had been warned that his presence was detected. He had almost reached safety in New Alkebulan when he had been captured. His captors were initially more brutal than he had ever dreamed. They beat and kicked him furiously, viciously, and continuously with fists, feet, clubs, and chains. Fortunately, he was able to protect his face. He hoped that his lack of facial scars during his conversation with Amma had helped to allay her suspicions. Indeed, when Joshua had been alerted that it was he who had been captured, the beating and torture stopped, and he was treated much better because of Joshua's orders.

Obadele watched Jomo come back into the room after he and Amma had completed their conversation. Jomo had stepped into the next room to allow Obadele to speak privately with her. When Jomo saw Obadele on his knees, he rushed over to help Obadele back into the seat.

"What happened?" Jomo asked.

Obadele sighed, "Man!! I never realized that deception was so draining. No wonder Horde seems so weary and jaded. Their lifestyle of deception exhausts them. I almost lost consciousness."

Obadele gratefully accepted Jomo's help but winced as Jomo firmly grasped him under his arms. He had six fractured ribs. As he settled in the chair awaiting the Healer, he and Jomo discussed the situation. They were close to agreement on what the best strategy would be but were both concerned about how to present it to the Council. Obadele knew that they had to be very careful because his cousin-brother, Kofi, would use this opportunity to further push his "Final Solution."

Kofi was the grandson of Baba Kamau, Nana Ade's brother. Kofi and Obadele were the same age and had been friendly rivals in everything during their youth. They both attributed their rivalry as one of the main factors in their attainment of excellence in their chosen fields. They loved and enjoyed each other's company but had great philosophical differences.

Kofi had become a great warrior and had earned a place on the Council early in his life, even earlier than Obadele. In fact, he had been the youngest person ever to sit on the Council. He had perfected his war skills while Obadele pursued further education in Linguist training. Despite their closeness and great affection for each other, Obadele and Kofi were worlds apart in their philosophy regarding the Horde. Kofi felt that the Horde should be systematically and aggressively hunted and captured. He thought that each Horde should be offered the opportunity to take Pex. If they refused, Kofi was in favor of performing what he called extermination. In fact, Kofi had engineered the institution as part of his solution. Humanity had been presented with the dilemma of what to do with captured Horde. The idea of re-starting prisons was not appealing since StoryTellers had taught that prisons had been used as weapons against Human Wholeness during the Maafa and only served to worsen already bad situations. It was undesirable to put so many Horde together in an environment so ripe for brutality. Kofi had attempted to convince the

Council to sentence captured Horde to Pex therapy involuntarily with weekly mandatory monitoring by several known and unknown Humans.

Obadele disagreed strenuously on every level and could use several aspects of TheStorical precedent as his reasons. He knew from discussion with Amma and Kwame and from his own research that during the early days of the Maafa, Horde religious groups gained Human converts by offering similar choices, conversion or death. Because Wholeness had been so damaged, many Humans could not see that they were being offered an empty substitute for their spirituality, which Horde called religion. This led to distrust and when Humanity regained control of Heart, the eventual destruction of the religions among Humanity.

Obadele also wanted to avoid the "Big Brother" monitoring and interference in every aspect of life so common during the Maafa. He felt that there must be a middle ground, a basis for coexistence and cooperation between Human and Horde, although he didn't know what that was. This was one of the reasons that he aggressively championed Aset and Jay's experiments.

Before Obadele and Jomo could agree on a strategy, the door alarm rang, and the Healer entered. Although somewhat in awe of the legendary Obadele Omowale, the Healer was efficient and began gathering the necessary information. His evaluation took almost thirty minutes. Obadele had numerous bruises and contusions all over his body and the six fractured ribs, but fortunately he had suffered no internal injuries. The healing ritual and treatment took another twenty minutes. Obadele felt much better at the end of the ceremony and treatment. He slept for almost two hours and awakened refreshed and feeling brand new. Jomo was still standing in the darkened room. Another person was there also.

He stared through sleepy eyes at the new silhouette. As his eyes cleared, he made out the features of the new person. She was a tall, stately, beautiful nut-brown woman with thickly locked salt and pepper hair that hung just below her shoulders. She had a concerned expression on her face and stared at him as if she was trying to read his thoughts. He finally said, "Hotep, Nzinga."

## Nzinga

Nzinga felt fortunate that she was in Menefer when Jomo's call reached her. She enjoyed traveling over New Alkebulon and was frequently away from her home in Menefer. She and Jomo sat across from Obadele and as Jomo described Obadele's experience and findings in Europa, she struggled to remain level headed. She had lost a husband and son during the Horde's attacks on New Atlantis and was shocked that they were already preparing for another assault. She didn't think that she could emotionally survive the loss of her beloved son-in-law Obadele or deal with Amma's grief without falling prey to her own weaknesses. Although she heard his greeting, the resounding nature of her thoughts seemed to paralyze her, and she sat transfixed, as if glued to the seat, staring at her beloved son-in-law who she loved like the son that she had lost.

She looked at Obadele as if it was the first time that she had seen him. He was an intense, highly intelligent, focused and yet simple man. He deeply loved and was completely dedicated to his people and his family. In this, he was a perfect match for Amma, who had the same qualities and priorities. Nzinga had remembered hoping that the Elder investigation would prevent them from marrying. She had loved Obadele and his siblings since they were babies. Their mothers had been her best friends since childhood. She also absolutely adored her daughter. Amma was the living embodiment of the proverb handed down from the Ancestors that said, "Children are the reward of life." Amma had been a perfect daughter. She hadn't felt that Amma and Obadele would be able to create a good union because of their dedication to Humanity. She had been surprised when the Elders allowed their marriage but was very pleased with their happiness. She was happy to have been wrong. Now that they were almost ready to start a family, she was again a little uneasy, but after making their marriage the success it had been for the past ten years, she was much more comfortable. She felt that if anyone could blend children into their lives, it was Amma and O.

"Well, what are we going to do with that Joshua person." she finally asked, to no one in particular.

Jomo and Obadele looked at each other. Jomo shrugged slowly. Obadele answered honestly, "I don't know. The Council will decide whether we prepare a defense or invade Europa and use a defensive offense."

Nzinga nodded, her locks covering her face. Even though she was a Healer, she had always been fascinated with Protectors. Her late husband, Kweku, had been a Protector, and her son, Mena, had been in training to be a Protector when he was killed. She had read the Protector literature and understood much of the theory.

"I'll wager that Kofi wants to invade," she said after a long pause.

Before Obadele or Jomo could reply, there was a knock at the door.

# CHAPTER TWO

## *The Plan of Aggression*

### <u>Joshua</u>

Sometimes Joshua couldn't understand the hatred he had for Humans. The ferocity sometimes even scared him. At times that he considered periods of weakness (that he would never admit to), he wished that he didn't hate them so much. However, he realized that his hatred sustained him. He was rarely concerned with where it took him, but he always went "there" freely. He rarely regretted his actions in pursuit of the fruits of hatred.

He peered at his reflection in the large glass of grog that he was drinking. His blonde hair was long, reaching below his shoulders, which made his receding hairline more pronounced. His long sideburns framed his pale pink face, and his thick mustache obscured his razor thin lips. His eyes seemed weary, even to him.

He had been a brilliant military-oriented scientist before giving his life to the single-minded pursuit of Horde dominance on Heart. He had been born into a Loyalist family in Menefer. Both his parents had been Basic Educators, and he had lived among Humans most of his early life. He had even at one time considered some Humans to be friends, such as Adwoa and Agyi Omowale and Osei and Opuku Buah. Nzinga Asantewa had been one of his favorite teachers.

However, he had always felt an uneasiness, a type of wanderlust. He never knew what he was feeling until he met an old Horde man wandering around New Arlantis who, though uneducated, partially blind, and cripple, convinced him that his uneasiness was being caused because he was suppressing his true Horde nature. He struggled with the old man's teachings for several years because his parents had taught him that Humans and Horde could and should live together peacefully. They believed that the natural aggressiveness of the Horde was a primitive trait that could be voluntarily controlled. How wrong they were! The old man, known simply as Carlos, had taught him to forget the Pex and give in to his aggressiveness, controlling only its expression but not its existence. Now, as leader of the Horde, free to give vent to all his violent urges, his sexual deviancies, and his greed, he rarely felt the earlier uneasiness. He did not feel perfectly comfortable, but it was a different type of discomfort, a discomfort that suited him because it actually gave him comfort.

By the time he completed his education in pure applied scientific research, he had been an agent of the government in Europa for almost five years. Before he physically defected to Europa, he managed to supply them with a large amount of valuable information that proved damaging to Humanity and helpful to the success of the Horde guerilla attacks.

He had done much of the crucial initial research in cloning and *in vivo* vitalitygenesis (creating life in the laboratory). When his research was stopped by the Human Council, because its basic theory and premise went against The Way, he had had enough. He took his research to Europa, became politically active and rose rapidly through the ranks. Because of the difficulty that he encountered in creating life, he had developed a respect for life that was rare among the Horde. Yet, he became a revered figure among his chosen people, and his reputation was, in fact, bigger than life. His known commitment to the Horde and his brutality were legendary.

There was a microscopically tiny area in an obscure part of the back of his mind that regretted his alienation with life. In weak moments (again, that he would never admit to), he even regretted not being able to know and have a relationship with his daughter. He felt that it had been a stroke of genius to rape and attempt to impregnate the Omowale twins. He struck several blows at once -he insulted their father, he paraded his perceived dominance and superiority over Humanity, and he attempted to break their spirits so that future Omowale generations would be weak. He knew that the first and primary source of strength and knowledge for children was from their mothers. He had killed two of his most dangerous opponents  (he realized at a deep level that he could not truthfully call them enemies) and had planted a Mulat into the Omowale clan that he hoped would be a weak link because of her mixed heritage. He would never admit that much of his emotional makeup was based on jealousy and left-over baggage.

As a youth, he had loved Adwoa Omowale but had been spurned repeatedly by her. Although she had always been kind to him, she firmly refused to even undergo an Elder Investigation to see if they were compatible. He blamed her father, Ade Omowale and began to hate the entire Omowale family. Shortly after his final proposal to undergo an Elder investigation for marriage had been refused, he met Carlos. How dare Adwoa say that she wanted them to be "just friends." He never even considered that the Elder investigation would probably have denied the marriage. When Adwoa chose Osei Buah, he was furious. How dare someone he had considered "friend" steal the love of his life. Carlos, unknown to Joshua, knew of these events and used them to convert Joshua from Loyalist to the epitome of Horde.

Even though Joshua openly stated his belief in a Supreme Creator, he subconsciously felt (as did most Horde), that as technical innovations and scientific advancements continued, Horde-kind could achieve the status of gods.

His god, Yah, was a jealous, vengeful and chauvinistic male deity who was said to severely punish whole families, even innocent, unborn children generations later, for the transgressions of one member. Joshua tried to model his practice of power on the religious model of his god.

As he planned the attack, he regretted that Obadele Omowale had been allowed to escape. He realized. that Obadele had probably learned of their intentions and that knowledge would eliminate the element of surprise in his planned attacks. However, characteristic of traditional Horde leadership, he had planned the campaign carefully and for a long term basis. Equally characteristic of Horde leadership, he had tunnel vision. He, like other Horde leaders, had difficulty in understanding or caring about the effects of their plan on those who they considered unimportant or expendable. Joshua intended to destroy all Humans once and for all even if he destroyed the environment and made it unsuitable for anyone to live there. He also wanted to wipe all Loyalists off the face of Heart, even though he knew that this would include killing his parents.

He was strangely ambiguous about Mulats and deep down in his subconscious, he really did not want to kill them. He always told himself that he didn't know why this ambiguity existed. He never consciously connected this ambiguity with his constant conscious readiness to publically deny that he had a Mulat child.

Overall, however, he was very happy with himself. He had united the main Horde factions (or "nations") under his leadership. This not only made him one of the most powerful and influential beings on Heart but the most powerful Horde leader ever. He could effectively attack several targets at once, regardless of geographical location. Other Horde leaders had led small groups or bands of Horde and performed hit and run guerilla raids on various Human settlements and even some cities. Although diabolically destructive, he felt that they never achieved much major success. He was determined to etch his name in Horde History (and the so-called TheStory of Humans) by dealing a blow so powerful to Humans that those who did survive would always be subjected to the control of the Horde.

His second-in-command, John Paul, a much younger man, had been the leader of the second largest nation, ThreeKay, which was adjacent to the Southern part of New Alkebulan. When it came to pure hatred of Humans, John was second to none. John and his predecessors in ThreeKay had wreaked havoc on New Atlantis for generations. Sometimes the raids were logistically ill-advised, and the Horde losses were unacceptable to a thinking person, but they were being led by their emotions rather than their thoughts. Joshua would change that mistake.

John saw in Joshua someone who shared his hatred of Humans and had the advantage of having lived among them. Joshua helped to clear up many of the tales about humans that were part of Horde folklore. Joshua had used this information to get John to join him. This was a brilliant achievement and was a tribute to Joshua's leadership skills.

The Northernmost nation, Asia, reluctantly joined him when they realized that ThreeKay had joined with New Europa. Asia was numerically less populous than either nation, and their leaders were convinced that if they didn't join with the Horde, they had no chance of survival. Asia was an unusual place. The people were neither Human nor Horde. Most of its inhabitants had a golden complexion and only wanted to be left alone. Unfortunately, this continuous war between Horde and Human always seemed to pull them in. They got along very well with Humans but were vulnerable to Horde.

The geographical territory of Asia was larger than Europa and ThreeKay combined, but their population was much less than half of even ThreeKay. This was related to a number of factors: the first was several large population centers in which 90% of the population lived. They were concentrated in seven large cities. Because of the cold climate in most of Asia, most people lived up South, where the climate was less severe. Many Asians had gradually migrated into New Alkebulan and had co-mingled with Humanity and Loyalists. In New Alkebulan, they felt that they were a part of a just society that valued them and were willing to be fully immersed and integrated into Human civilization. Those Asians who remained in Asia favored neither Human nor Horde, but were, of necessity, pragmatic. The population centers bordered on and, more often than not, were almost surrounded by New Europa. They had no choice but to forge relationships with the Horde for their own survival. Their leader, Po Li, was a brilliant yet pragmatic strategist.

John walked into the room where Joshua was deep in thought. He said curtly, "I apologize for my lateness, Josh, but I couldn't get away from my third wife. I'm ready to start the interrogation of Obadele Omowale." As he pronounced the name, a sneer brightened his face, and despite his attempts, a look of excitement flashed across it too.

Joshua looked down at the floor and sighed loudly. He then stood up and grabbed the smaller man by the collar and slammed his body violently against the wall. John felt himself being lifted and realized that his feet dangled twelve centimeters above the floor. "Don't you ever call me 'Josh' again," Joshua growled. Josh had been Adwoa's name for him, and he didn't want to be reminded. Although he would never admit it, the searing pain of Adwoa's rejection remained fresh. How did John know? Did he know? He stared into John's steely gray eyes for several minutes and smiled. When he released the younger man, John's knees almost buckled when his feet were back on the floor. Joshua then said, "Of course you won't," as he smoothed John's wrinkled collar, with. an icy stare accompanying his chilling smile. He then said, matter-of-factly, "He escaped. I should really apologize to you for not alerting you sooner, to save you from rushing here, taking a needless trip."

John's blank expression hid the terror and disappointment that he felt. He feared Joshua more than he had ever feared anything or anyone, and he loved Joshua as much as he feared him. He wondered what he had said to trigger so violent a response. He was a sadist and loved inflicting pain. He also felt that a good sadist was also a good masochist and had trained himself to love physical pain. He even carved patterns on his body with a knife in addition to the more than thirty tattoos and piercings that he had. He felt let down at not having the chance to break that uppity Nag, Obadele Omowale. He dared not reveal his true feelings to Joshua, however, and without changing his facial expression said, "That's OK. I needed to come here anyway to finish some research. How did he escape?" He knew that Joshua valued research and hoped that his statement would distract the older man and win him some "brownie points" with the cruel scientist-leader.

Joshua turned his back on the younger man and walked slowly towards his desk. He replied casually, "He obviously had some help. I've given the order that everyone who came in contact with him be killed. There is at least one traitor in our inner guard. We can't take the necessary time or effort, now, to flush these turkeys out of hiding. The coming executions will be a lesson for them all."

John smiled. Despite his fear of Joshua, he admired his brilliantly ruthless nature. Widespread knowledge of the mass executions surrounding Omowale's escape would drive many traitorous Loyalists deeper into hiding, neutralizing them for a while, at least. It would also make non-traitorous Horde more careful to avoid the appearance of being a traitor.

Joshua looked at the younger man. He said casually, "We need to regain control of Heart. Everything is too orderly. There's no real excitement. It's just too peaceful. I'm bored!"

John listened intently. He knew that Joshua was one of the foremost Rememberers of the Glory Days when Horde had controlled Heart. He never tired of hearing about it. His eyes glazed in anticipation of more information.

"When we had control," Joshua continued, "Every day was exciting. Competition existed in every facet of life. We were like puppet masters. We controlled all the playing fields, and although we knew the outcome of each contest, it was still intoxicating, just watching it."

John asked, "If we were in so much control, how did we lose Heart?"

Joshua glared at the younger man, "We have not lost Heart!"

It infuriated Joshua when young Horde, ignorant of their own history, refused to think positively about their past and future. It mattered little what the actual facts were, but he wanted them to think positively, not accurately.

During the era that the Humans called The Maafa, Horde had perfected the methods of colonization of information not only about the past but about all things. When Humanity had begun to regain knowledge of their true past, the Horde were able to stall by accusing Humans of what Horde themselves had done for years, fabricating "feel-good history" and reporting "fake news". When the necessary critical mass of Humans realized that the so-called "feel-good history" was their true past, their "Story", they began institutionalizing rituals and celebrations that helped bring them back to themselves. This was especially dangerous to Horde control when the Horde-created "religions" were exposed for what they were, false interpretations of Human culture, using a

Horde man as the image of the deity. This proved to be extremely effective in controlling Humanity because their ignorance of their own innate spirituality allowed them to invest spiritual values in the religions that were not really there. The Horde had been so supremely confident that it was too late for Humans to stop their own mental self-destruction that consequently, it was too late for them to adjust when they realized what the Humans were doing. Even so, because of the Horde spiritual limitations, they never fully understood what happened.

They began to criminalize Humans while subjecting them to poverty. They understood that poverty stifled most analytic and creative thoughts because of the drive to simply survive. As a result, this poverty and survival instinct also increased the frequency of crimes of survival, such as theft and trafficking in illegal substances. This allowed them to inflict repressive laws and excessive punishments on Humans who were merely attempting to survive. There was the constant threat of state-sanctioned Horde-on-Human violence, especially by those whose stated function was to "protect and serve." These constant terroristic threats of violence damaged many Humans psychologically and even changed chemical balances in their neuro systems that induced a disease state. There seemed to be a Pineal Insufficiency state that was even partially resistant to Pex. Through epigenetic mechanisms, these frustrations frequently overwhelmed pineal function and increased the occurrence of short bursts of violent acts. In short, Humans became Horde-like.

Humans had also developed aberrant loyalties. Because of blind unthinking and uncritical belief in Horde-created religious doctrine and unquestioned acceptance of the myth of citizenship in nation-states totally controlled by Horde, many Humans willingly participated in their own destruction. Some Humans eventually realized what they were doing but continued to work against their own people. When Humans regained control of Heart, these traitors were isolated and ostracized and died alone in infamy. What the Horde hadn't counted on was the resurgence of Human consciousness and "peoplehood" and the realization, by Humans, finally that some violence would be necessary if they were to be successful in their efforts to better their condition. The Horde were caught unprepared, lost the war and lost control of Heart in the process.

"Well," Joshua thought, "It will be different this time. I'll see to it that it is".

# CHAPTER THREE

*The Counter Plan*

## Amma

When the hotel door opened, all Amma could see was Obadele. She rushed into his arms, and they both shed tears of joy. She held on to him as if she was having a tug-of-war with all the Horde forces on Heart, and Obadele was the center. She felt safe in his arms as she always did. Her eyes were tightly shut, and she gave up all her senses to the warmth and smell of her beloved "other half". She loved the feel and scent of him, and she especially loved the rhythm of his heartbeat. She was ready to stay there in his arms forever when she heard a familiar voice being cleared. She remembered that there were other people in the room, but did not feel embarrassed. She opened her eyes, her head against his chest, and smiled when the first person she saw was her mother.

"Mama! What are you doing here?" She asked, still clinging to Obadele but reaching one arm to her mother.

"Nana Jomo told me that Obadele had been captured by those beasts," replied Nzinga as she held the outstretched hand of her daughter. Amma's other hand still clutched Obadele as if he were trying to get away from her. She refused to lose the touch of him, even for a minute, not even to embrace her mother.

Amma, happy and secure in her husband's arms and her mother's touch, stifled a mischievous smile, despite the obvious gravity of the situation. Since the end of the eighteen month official mourning period after her father's funeral, her mother had traveled all over New Alkebulan and even to the Holy Land, Ta Ntr. During those travels, Amma had noticed that Nzinga and Jomo were spending more and more time together. Even though Jomo was several years younger than Nzinga, Amma was glad that her mother had apparently found a companion. Jomo was a good man. He, too, was alone. His wife, Asabi, had died from a mysterious infection widely believed to have been introduced by the Horde. The Horde had perfected the art of using science and technology to create increasingly horrible weapons of mass destruction.

As she squeezed Obadele tightly, she felt him flinch. Of course!! He had been being brave for her. He was hurt, after all. She reluctantly left the comfort and safety of his arms and looked at him.

Before she could speak, Kwame's deep voice boomed from the direction of the still open door, "Hotep, Big Brother."

Obadele glanced towards the familiar voice at the door and smild, "Almost everyone is here. Good! Hotep, L'il Fella."

Kwame, followed closely by Aset, quickly moved to where Amma was hanging on to her husband. They joined the embrace and formed a circle.

Nzinga and Jomo both smiled. It was good to see young people so loving and dedicated to each other.

When their emotions calmed, the six people sat at the large dining room table in the suite to hear Obadele's report. Obadele sat at one end, and Amma sat at the other, naturally assuming the role of co-hosts of the gathering.

"There's not much good news," Obadele said glumly. "New Europa and ThreeKay have joined forces and they're pressuring Asia to join them."

Amma and Aset gasped, almost in unison. They looked at each other. They had been inseparable for so many years that they frequently thought alike and reacted to things in the same way. They even finished each others' sentences. Ordinarily, when this happened, they would giggle girlishly, but neither felt like giggling since the very existence of Humanity was being threatened.

There was a long silence. Finally, Aset asked, "When will they attack?"

Obadele shrugged, "I don't know." He looked at Kwame and then at Amma and said, "I think they are going to do something based in their verion of TheStory."

Amma mindlessly corrected him, "They call it history."

Aset's mind started to reel. If there was to be another war so soon, Humanity's quest for Wholeness would be delayed, perhaps permanently. Wars brought all negative emotions to the surface and drove Wholeness away.

Jay had once asked her if Wholeness was truly needed since Wholy people could not defend themselves from Horde. He asked, "As desirable as it is to be Wholy, isn't the reason that Horde have prevailed during the Breakthrough Period of the Maafa, that Humans were unable to react because of the peacefulness and serenity of Wholeness?"

She had answered that true Wholeness enabled Humans to use a different set of weapons for defense; mental and spiritual weapons that would make physical violence unnecessary and obsolete. Before the Maafa, Wholy Humans were unaware of the true nature of the Horde and did not completely understand the true nature and potential of Wholeness until it was too late. She hadn't elaborated any further, and Jay had seemed satisfied with the answer.

Kwame broke the silence, interrupting his wife's thoughts and asked Obadele, "What do you mean? What TheStorical or historical information will they use?"

"I don't know," replied Obadele. "Maybe we should contact our Loyalist agents in New Europa to find out."

Jomo spoke for the first time since Amma, Aset and Kwame had entered the room, "I think that's too risky. We've already lost three important high placed Loyalist agents who helped Obadele escape. Joshua killed everyone who had come in contact with Obadele, trying to plug up his information leak. Fortunately, we have more agents in place, but it's riskier to try to contact them now. We need to discuss this in the Council and involve Kofi."

Obadele sighed. Military strategy was the area that Kofi excelled in. Kofi had been taught by Nana Ade and by his own grandfather, Baba Kamau and was the most brilliant strategist and the finest Warrior on Heart.

Kofi and his best friend, Kweku Ige, would contribute significantly to the discussion of strategy.

Nzinga noted the time and used her seniority to break up the gathering. They were coming uncomfortably close to discussing politics outside the Council, which was forbidden for Council members and affiliates except in strictly defined situations. The current situation would soon qualify but had to be voted as such by the Council. It was very late and she knew that everyone present could have been there all night talking and enjoying each other's company. She reminded them that the matters at hand would be discussed at the

Council meeting the next day and they all needed to be as fresh as possible.

Aset and Kwame went to the registration desk to get a suite and Jomo went to his Council quarters. Nzinga was the last to leave. She watched everyone say their goodbyes before she embraced her daughter and son-in-law (Amma had again embraced her husband and wouldn't release her hold on him). Nzinga silently kissed her daughter on both cheeks and kissed her son-in-law on the forehead before going to her apartment.

## Amma and Obadele

When everyone had left, Obadele turned on the audio system and he and Amma settled into the love seat Amma was careful not to leave her husband's embrace. They both favored rhythms, although they also liked tones and harmonics. Drumming had reached a level of sophistication never before known in Human TheStory, as had instrumental, vocal and spoken music. Rhythms could be adjusted to fit any mood and were frequently used by Healers as advanced therapy. Colors that matched the moods caused by the rhythms flooded the room.

The rhythm that Obadele chose was a slow and sensuous rhythm similar to the rhythm formerly called "bolero" that had a subtle but definite back-beat that stimulated the nerve endings at the base of the spine, the first two chakras. Amma smiled and shivered in anticipation when she recognized the rhythm. It was their favorite lovemaking rhythm. That rhythm or a variation of it had played almost constantly during the four-week period of seclusion after their wedding week.

She looked intently at Obadele and smiled. He stood and stared back into her eyes. He held his hand out to her, and she slowly stood up while reaching for his hand. He folded her in his arms, and they danced as she cuddled closer to him. Again, she felt safe and secure. They danced for several minutes with her head cradled in the curve between his neck and shoulder. She tilted her head up to look at him. They lost themselves in each other's eyes for several more minutes, and then he kissed her lips gently. Even though the touch of their lips was light, Amma's lips burned as if they had been ignited by a volcano.

The next kiss was longer and more urgent. They undressed each other quickly--reluctant for their lips and tongues to lose contact. When they were both completely nude, they sank slowly to the floor. Their hands explored the familiar territory of the other's body, and the touch of hands was followed by hot, urgent kisses that followed their hands. When their bodies finally joined together as one, they were both surprised at the gentleness of their lovemaking, despite the torrid urgency of their need.

Afterward, they lay in each other's arms for a long while, until their breathing slowed and became even. Giggling, they collected their clothing, put the room back in order, and got into bed. Amma noted that Obadele did not change the rhythm playing on the audio system. In bed, they faced each other and embraced, their bodies in total contact, lying together for minutes before starting to talk. Each felt so comfortable and so natural as if they had been born together. In many ways, they seemed more like telepathic identical twins than husband and wife.

Obadele said softly, "They call this new Horde Alliance 'The United Confederacy'. It's very bothersome."

"Yes, it is," Amma replied. "This has the potential to become worse than the Maafa." She sat up abruptly, her eyes wide, "Did you say that this offensive will be based in their story, History? Perhaps the word Confederacy is indeed the link to their past. It seems too simple, almost incomplete."

Obadele nodded absently, her scent exciting him again, especially with the relentless erotic rhythmic pulsations emitting from the octophonic speakers in the room and bed, stimulating his lower chakras.

Before he could begin to touch, stroke and kiss those places on her that he knew were sensitive, she said grimly, "The Confederacy was the name of the government of Horde during the era called the Civil War in old America. This was when two factions of Horde disagreed on the methods of our dehumanization and enslavement. One side favored physical brutality and total enslavement. In contrast, the other favored creating what our Ancestors called' The Illusion of Inclusion', making us think that we were free while controlling our minds, our thoughts, our aspirations and our physical and emotional environments. This may be the clue, the historical basis for their attack."

Her words, spoken so plainly, cut deeply into his psyche like a machete. His amorous thoughts disappeared. She was the expert in the Maafa, and during the years of their relationship, he had learned a great deal from her about that era in Human TheStory. Obadele believed very strongly in the ultimate victory of Maat (order) over Isfet (disorder). He had no doubt that he was a soldier in the forces of Maat. In view of these recent occurrences, he couldn't help but wonder if

Humanity had displeased the Creator and Ancestors. Was Humanity being punished by reliving the Maafa? He verbalized these thoughts to Amma.

Before answering, Amma snuggled closer to her husband, her curves filling the empty spaces in his body. She reflected on the Maafa. For many years, because of the painful and shameful memories, Humanity had not systematically studied the Maafa. What they did study was superficial, dealt with platitudes and was often misleading and occasionally false. However, with the benefit of Third Eye Vision (intuitive foresight), TheStorical evaluation (hindsight), and the So Dayi (mature three dimensional) analysis of both; as well as the realization that it could happen again unless they faced it and studied it thoroughly, they had finally realized the true extent of the Maafa. Even then, there had been an evolution of theories about the nature, and even the actual existence, of the Maafa. Many older Storytellers had believed that the Maafa had ended when formal physical enslavement of Humans had stopped. That view gave way to the opinion that the legal system that ended Heart-wide Apartheid ended the Maafa. The next theory in this evolution of theories held that the Maafa ended when there seemed to be genuine positive change in the hearts and minds of the masses of Horde towards Humanity.

It was currently widely accepted by Storytellers that the Maafa ended when Human values, ethics, morals, cultural mores, standards of beauty and perfection regained primacy on planet Heart.

The final revolution that had led to the end of the Maafa had not been completely bloodless, but the overall peacefulness of it magnified the superiority of the Human

Way. Unfortunately, most of the bloodshed was that of Humans being attacked in cowardly fashion by Horde.

The Revolution started with a concept called Pan-Humanism that was designed to defeat the confusion that had been brilliantly created by the Horde in their "divide and conquer" strategy. Pan-Humanism held that all Humans all over the planet were the same regardless of the culture imposed upon them. The Horde had successfully convinced most Humans that each group who lived in different Horde-defined geopolitical arenas was different. This had worked very well for a long time. Many Humans mindlessly accepted Horde culture, languages, philosophy, religion, standards of beauty as the universal norm. This damaged them even more because they even fought each other in defense of the Horde systems of government and culture. In fact, a time arose when Horde had Humans doing almost all their fighting. It was as if Humans had become the action figures on a game board or protagonists on a video game.

Human leaders who had emerged went through a now well-known progression of paradigms. The leaders at the beginning of the Maafa felt that the Horde were Humans who just looked a little differently from Humans. When they realized that Horde were not the same as Humans, the leaders fought to keep the Horde away and be left alone. Unfortunately, by the time they had reached this realization, it was too late to be successful at anything but complete wanton destruction of everything related to Horde, but this was not Humanly and thus not even seriously considered.

The next group of Human leaders tried to "hold it together". They attempted to establish separate institutions just for Humans without Horde influence. This was difficult because so many Humans felt that Horde needed to be included in every Human activity. The Horde response was to raise up Human leaders who were given all possible publicity while suppressing access to information about the separatist (maroon) Humans. This was diabolically successful, and the false theory of Horde-Human "cooperation" gained dominance in the minds of the Human public in a system called "integration".

For many years, Humanity was fooled into striving for a deliberately elusive and impossible dream of a Heart where all Humans and all Horde lived together for the "common good".

Finally, some Humans awakened and saw Horde for what they were. It was then that Pan-Humanism truly began. The factions of Humans that had been artificially created by the Horde's divide-and-conquer methods slowly began to eliminate the many geographic/class/complexion designations that had separated them. It was only then that Humanity brought Maat back to Heart, which was followed by the discovery of Pex.

Amma and Obadele alternately talked and made love for hours before they fell asleep in each other's arms. They awakened the following morning and made love again, this time very slowly. Again, they were surprised by the intensity of their passion.

When they finally tore themselves from the bed, they each became quiet, thinking about the pending Council meeting.

# CHAPTER FOUR

## *The Council Meeting*

After a quick breakfast, Amma, Obadele, Kwame and Aset piled into Kwame's copter, which was also used as a land car and rode to the meeting. The ride to the council chamber in the land car was eerily silent. Whenever the Omowales got together, there was almost always lots of laughter. They all enjoyed the company of their family and did not hesitate to demonstrate their deep love for each other. Their silence gave voice to the powerful mixed emotions that were building up in them.

When they arrived, the sounds in the Council Chamber were strangely subdued. People laughed loudly when greeting old friends, but there was an expectant, almost fearful atmosphere. The seats in the chamber were arranged in a semi-circular arrangement, each row one step higher than the previous row. Most people stood in the area at the bottom, where the podium was located and conversed in small groups. The Omowales sat on the front, bottom-most row, to the left of the podium, the place reserved for those presenting, being honored, or highly respected. Nzinga was already there waiting for them.

Jomo, sitting alone at the desk where the podium was located, in front of the assembled people, stood erect and, in a loud voice, said, "Agoo!". He chanted the last syllable holding it for several seconds.

The assembled women and men responded, "Amee," and quietly went to their seats. The silence thundered like a thousand cannons.

Jomo poured Libation and invoked the Ancestors' presence and wisdom more powerfully than usual. The accompanying drums were hypnotic, and almost everyone in the chamber felt the presence of the Ancestors. Jomo paused and looked into each face, left to right, before speaking again. There were about thirty-five women and men present, mostly Humans, but a few Loyalists and Mulats were in the room. The deliberateness of Jomo's movements raised the tension to an almost unbearable level.

Again, in a loud voice, though softer than his previous pronouncements, Jomo started to speak quite eloquently, "My dear sisters and brothers. As always, it is pleasant to greet you. However, the cause for this gathering is not pleasant."

He again paused and looked around the room. He lowered his voice as he seemed to crouch into a coiled position and said dramatically, through clenched teeth, "The Horde will attack us again soon".

His body and facial expression seemed to relax after relieving his soul of that terrible information. He continued, "We know that we must prepare a defense but what kind of defense? Are we to do anything else? If so, what else should we do?"

Without hesitation, a youthful appearing man sitting next to Obadele raised his hand and stood, his bearing regal and his back straight. He was a tall man with a round, almost cherubic face. He was slender, yet had well-developed muscles. His complexion was that of rich deep chocolate, his skin smooth as silk. His short black hair was locked. Jomo nodded, and the young man left his seat and stepped to the center of the room, next to Jomo. He turned and faced the assembled Elders. He was dressed in a simple tan dashiki and matching pants. He wore the purple kufi of a Protector. He was slightly taller than Jomo. By the time he reached the center of the room, his expression had changed, now concerned yet stubborn.

He spoke slowly, his deep voice forceful, yet respectful, "I ask permission of my Elders to speak."

Jomo again nodded, and without expression, said, "Speak, Kofi Omowale."

The young man took a deep breath and began to speak earnestly in a soft voice. The tenor in his tone matched the earnestness with which he spoke. He started, "For a long time, I have favored extermination of the Horde."

There was an immediate soft but brief murmur in the room. It had been widely rumored that Kofi Omowale favored extermination, but few people had actually heard it directly from him. Kofi continued, "It is important that the Council realize that the extermination solution was mine alone and not the opinion of anyone in my family. In fact," he said, looking pointedly at the front row of the section to his left where Nzinga, Obadele, Amma, Kwame, and Aset were sitting, "Many of my family members have been trying to dissuade me from this opinion."

He dropped his gaze to the floor but quickly looked up and looked at Jomo, "They have been partially successful."

Amma and Aset gasped softly and looked at each other. They had both given tremendous effort during family gatherings and informal visits to win Kofi over to their view. They tried not to include Obadele and Kwame because of their long-standing rivalry and the male habit of injecting excess testosterone into simple situations, making them more complicated than they had to be.

Kofi spoke again, "The basis for my solution was not hatred or bitterness. Those emotions are more characteristic of Isfet than Maat. It seemed to me to be quite reasonable that if there is a recurrent painful problem that does not respond to any solution that is tried, the best way to solve the problem is to eliminate it, to excise it. My family has convinced me that extermination, a solution that might deal with the problem superficially, has too much anti-Maat baggage, and the karma would be terrible. Although now I don't think that blanket extermination is the answer, I would favor establishing voluntary reserves under our control, perhaps in Asia or in the far down-north part of Alkebulan, that are impenetrable and inescapable for Horde who still refuse Pex, even after a suitable trial. That way, they can live their own lives yet not be a constant threat to the existence of Humanity on Heart," he paused dramatically, "as they have been for the past several millennia."

I have learned from my cousin sister Aset that they may even still evolve to where we are and develop their own Pineal Extract if left alone. This, I feel, is the best of all possible results. The worst that can happen is that they wipe themselves out, which would be their own doing. That latter occurrence would still work to our benefit and have less anti-Maatian baggage."

He paused again and then continued. "I have located some mountain ranges in the far down North area, that have the cold weather and snow that Horde love so dearly. If we give them simple tools of survival rather than weapons of aggression and mass destruction, and if we implement an environmental supplementation, we will be safe and free from the defensive thought of potential violence that drain us of so much Pineal Extract. At the same time, the Horde will be safe and happy. If we can forge a cooperative relationship with the Asians, this 'preserve' could be located in Asia. This would give us a common goal of survival. The Asians would have another reason to ally with us." He looked around at the assemblage and walked back to his seat.

Amma couldn't believe her ears! It was as if he had read her mind several hours ago. She raised her hand quickly before several other hands were raised. Jomo beckoned to her. She stood and asked the Elders for permission to speak. When permission was granted, she leveled her gaze at Kofi and said, "Kofi speaks the truth."

Even though another murmur started, she continued, starting to speak before the murmur subsided and feeling the eyes of her husband on her, "If left to their own devices, they will, indeed, survive or perish. I have two questions about the suggestion given by my cousin brother, however."

Without looking, she could feel Obadele relax. He had been initially unsure of where she was headed.

"If we knowingly place the Horde in a position that we know is possibly fatal, would that not be anti-Maatian?" She continued, "Many Horde, even children may die. We cannot forcibly take Horde children from their parents...it would be too Horde-like, wouldn't it?" She hesitated and looked around the room. She said, "It would be a perfect solution if it were not for our collective vow to 'Do Maat'." How is the solution that Kofi suggests Maatic, and how does it demonstrate reciprocity?"

A deep and low murmur filled the room as Amma again paused.

"The second question is," she continued, "how do we convince the Horde to move to the area Kofi suggests in Far Down North? I am very sure that they will not even seriously consider this alternative. Do we then become the aggressors in what is sure to be a violent confrontation?"

She sat down before getting an answer. There was a scattering of applause. It was less than she had expected. Kofi had prepared well and had done his behind the scenes work effectively, she thought, horrified. Had Kofi been practicing politics outside of the Council without the formal blessing of the Council?

That latter realization hit her like a sledgehammer! He was behaving like a politician!! Even though she had already taken her seat when the thought passed, she felt faint momentarily, as if she was going to pass out. Compromise of truth, destruction of harmony and elimination of reciprocity resulted from being a successful politician and were forbidden by the Maatic Code. Kofi had apparently met with some carefully selected members of the Council before the Council meeting, which effectively eliminated balance. She felt a profound sadness. She had no doubt that Kofi was sincere and actually thought that he was doing the right thing for the right reasons. She made a mental note to discuss this latest development with Aset. Together, they would find a way to make Kofi realize the serious breach of Maatian protocol that he had committed.

Lost in her thoughts, she suddenly became aware of the silence around her and looked over at Jomo. No one had spoken, and Jomo had assumed the position of Ka, standing straight, legs together with both arms fully extended upwards. The room was deathly quiet. Apparently, others had realized the breach also. She turned and looked at Kofi. His head was down, preventing eye contact. She closed her eyes.

Obadele stiffened in his seat, and she felt sick. His Protector training was obviously coming to the forefront! He was ready to attack or defend! She was afraid to open her eyes and find out what was happening but reluctantly opened them. Kofi had stood up again, and his friend Kweku was walking towards her. They had poorly concealed scowls on their faces. Kwame started to rise, but a barely perceptible touch by Obadele stopped him. She knew that even though Kwame was a storyteller, he was also an expert in martial arts because Nana Ade and Baba Kamau had both felt it important that their grandchildren qualify as experts in martial arts and weapons training. Their sister, Aisha, was also an expert martial artist, perhaps even better than Obadele, Kwame and Kofi.

When Kweku reached the front row and stood next to Kofi, Obadele effortlessly stood and embraced Kofi. She immediately realized that this was an offensive, as well as a defensive maneuver. He was effectively shielding her with his body and holding Kofi. He was also demonstrating to all, especially Kofi, his commitment to his cousin.

Obadele whispered to Kofi, "We will always be as one."

Kofi stopped in his tracks. He knew what Obadele was doing but still appreciated his public demonstration of support. Kofi started back up to the podium, intending to respond to Amma's subtle suggestions. He was furious at first, more at himself than at Amma, but was now more contrite. He appreciated Kweku's allegiance but made a mental note to help Kweku become a more independent thinker. He knew that Kweku was willing and ready to follow whatever lead that Kofi offered,

The Elders applauded at Kofi and Obadele's embrace. Tears welled in many eyes. They all knew and respected the Omowale family because of their long, multigenerational loyalty and service to Heart. They were also aware of the lifelong rivalry and philosophical differences between Kofi and Obadele. Many feared that these differences might cause a split in the Council and hence, in Heart. The embrace communicated to the Council that the Omowale Clan was still united despite the differences of opinion. They knew that Funtumireku/Denkymireku (the two crocodiles with one stomach, a symbol of unity even within diversity and disagreement) was powerfully in effect. This was the purest demonstration of Harmony and Righteousness that many had seen in many years.

Aset glanced at Kwame. The pride in his smile was almost palpable. He got up and joined the embrace. Obadele and Kofi made room for him, and the three men embraced for what seemed like an eternity with the applause of the Council roaring loudly in the background. There was a collective feeling that everything was going to be all right as long as the Omowales were together. Before dismissing the Council, Jomogave then limited permission to discuss the events and situation with each other in order to prepare for the next meeting.

## The Omowale Men

When the council meeting had ended, Obadele and Kofi agreed that the Omowale men should spend time together. They decided to have lunch together at Kofi's townhouse. Kofi had seen his wife, Fumi, leave the Council meeting with Aisha, who had been late and sat in the back of the chambers. He thought that they were going to go shopping or continuing the discussion at Aisha's hotel room. He had whispered in her ear that he and his cousin brothers would be at their house. She understood and nodded her agreement.

When the men arrived at Kofi and Fumi's house, they made themselves comfortable at the dining room table while Kofi prepared refreshments. He finally sat at the head of the table and looked at his cousin brothers silently.

As they sat sipping palm wine and eating fruit salad, Kwame watched Kofi and Obadele. There was no indication in either of them of any baggage left over from the meeting.

As three of the four surviving Omowales in their generation (Aisha was the fourth), they were all fully aware of their family's unique responsibility to Humanity. They represented the sixteenth generation of Omowales that had dedicated their lives to Humanity and to the achievement of Wholeness.

## The Omowale Women

After the meeting, Amma and Aset went to Amma's and Obedele's suite in Nkrumah Square. After entering, they both fell into chairs in the parlor. Feeling exhausted but relieved, they smiled at each other. Aset repeated a statement that she'd made to Amma many times, "We're married to greatness, my sister!!"

Amma gave her usual reply, "And so we are, my sister!!"

They giggled. Not just because the events that had occurred at the Council meeting had actually suggested that both statements were true, but because of the sheer joy of being together.

They were quiet. It was not an awkward silence because of their total comfort with each other. They both were deep in thought.

After ten minutes of silence, Amma, her eyebrows raised, indicating her seriousness, broke the silence, "You do realize that we still have a lot of work to do with Kofi?"

Aset nodded. Despite the obvious love and dedication that the Omowales had for each other, they were still far apart philosophically. It also occurred to her that Kofi might be upset with Amma for publically exposing him. She asked, "Where should we start?"

Amma replied, "I really don't know, but it seems to me that we won't know unless we speak with Kofi. He lives here in Menefer, so we should be able to reach him. The only question is timing. When should we contact him?"

Amma pondered the question. After a few minutes, she said, "They are all together now. We should wait and see whether we need to add to the conversation or do damage control."

There was a knock on the door.

Amma gave a puzzled look at Aset, "That was quick. I hope things didn't degenerate."

She opened the door and saw Nzinga, Fumi and Aisha smiling at her. Amma embraced her mother, then Aisha and Fumi, and Aset did the same. They all went into the kitchen and prepared tea before sitting around the circular table.

It was during the women's meeting that the germ for the strategy was conceived. The conversation was animated. Rarely did Amma, Aset, Nzinga, and Aisha have the opportunity to be alone with each other. When Fumi joined them, the circle was complete. They happily talked and laughed about everything that came to their minds. They discussed their husbands, their families, and Nzinga gave them a historical perspective.

Fumi was the first to mention the Council meeting. She looked at Amma and said, "I didn't want to mention this before, but at dinner yesterday, Kofi was so happy. He said that he felt like he was getting his family back."

Amma was surprised, "What do you mean, Fumi? He's always had his family."

"Well, his philosophy on dealing with the Horde, he called it "The Final Solution", was so different from the rest of the family that he felt estranged. You know how sensitive he is. He feels everything so deeply and really wants Umoja (unity) to reign supreme. He came back from the meeting saying that Umoja did reign, but with diversity. I think the Priest-Philosophers call it Funtumireku Denkymireku."

Aisha spoke up, "Actually, I don't think he really meant the full picture of his "Final Solution". He is intense, but I think he really wanted to jolt the Council and other Elders into quickly creating a solution."

Everyone looked at Aisha and then at Fumi. Fumi smiled. Although accomplished in her chosen area of music, she believed that each of the women in the room had more direct responsibility in dealing with the crisis than she had. She wasn't intimidated or resentful. She was comfortable in who she was and comfortable in her relationship with her sister family members. She looked at Amma again and said, "Aisha is right, I think. Kofi is a man of action and wanted the planners and strategizers to actively plan and strategize."

The word "strategy" jolted Aset. She almost jumped out of her seat and asked Aisha, "Have you ever met Joshua?"

Aisha's expression became grim, and the corners of her mouth twitched with tension. After a long pause, her features softened, and she relaxed. "No. He used to send e-messages to me when I was younger but stopped when I never answered."

Aset leaned eagerly forward, her eyes narrowing and her eyebrows almost meeting her eyelids, "You never told me about those messages, what did he say?"

Aisha looked puzzled. She answered slowly and deliberately, pronouncing each word carefully, looking deeply into Aset's eyes and trying to understand the reasons for the questions. "He wanted me to join him in Europa. He always said that because I was half-Horde, I could never be satisfied to "merely" be Human" (she drew out the word "merely" into almost a chant). She thought, "Perhaps I should consider that option. I could possibly get some helpful information."

Amma spoke up, "That's too risky, Aset. It might endanger Aisha, and her brothers would never allow it".

Nzinga, who had been listening quietly up to that point in the conversation, spoke up, "Whoa y'all." Y'all was an Ebonics word from the 19th, 20th and 21st centuries that she frequently used to describe Amma and Aset. "You three have always been able to read each others' minds. Slow up and enlighten us all so we can all be on the same page."

Aisha looked up at Nzinga and said, "They want me to somehow gain Joshua's confidence and go undercover into Europa."

Fumi looked worried. Her training did not deal with danger, and she didn't like what she was hearing. She asked, "Shouldn't Warriors and Protectors do those kinds of things?"

Aset answered, "Exactly. Because it was Aisha, his daughter, who is neither Warrior nor Protector, his suspicions might not be as high. Aisha is a highly trained martial artist and can take care of herself. She could find weaknesses in Horde defenses and other valuable information that might help us. We might possibly intercede without causing any major damage to ourselves or to the Horde. Think about it, the fact that he tried to establish contact with Aisha shows that he does have a soft spot for her, which might be exploited for our benefit.

Nzinga got up and walked to the window, quietly and deliberately, looking out at the city. The conversation stopped as each of the women watched her. She turned after a while and asked, "Suppose he has given himself totally over to the beastiality of the Horde Way?"

Amma answered before anyone else could speak, "We can have Aisha communicate with him for a while before she decides what to do. In that way, we can analyze his responses and decide whether the risk is worth taking. Actually, that reminds me that we should all also take some Warrior and Protector training."

Aset continued Amma's thought, "We cannot let Kwame, Obadele or Kofi know what is happening. They would never allow it. And even if they could be convinced, Joshua's predictable test to observe and gauge their reactions might warn him that something is amiss". She looked at Amma and then at Fumi. "Our men are decent, straightforward and honorable men. They are not practiced in deception. They are not two-faced hypocrites and would not be able to act surprised enough to convince Joshua. We must maintain what used to be called 'plausible deniability'."

Nzinga looked away again and spoke so softly that all the women strained to hear her words. "There is wisdom in the plan. However, I fear for Aisha. I also fear for your husbands' reactions when they find out that they have been deceived. We _must_ discuss this plan with Jomo. We cannot risk implementing it alone. We must also be as one in this in all details. Are we unanimous?"

Although these last statements hit the ladies like a sledgehammer, they all quietly agreed. The future of Heart and Humanity was at stake.

## The Other Council Meeting

Joshua marched into the large, drab gray room and stood at the head of a long rectangular table. He stood there silently and looked deeply into the eyes of each of the twelve men seated at the long table. He saw admiration, fear, arrogance, jealousy and hatred. These reactions stimulated a mixture of feelings in him. He felt emotions from pride to raw hatred and disgust. He knew that the only reason that he continued to stand as their leader was the respect that was borne, in great part, of their fear of him. Joshua had shown himself to be more thoughtfully vicious and creatively savage than any of them could ever have imagined.

He smiled inwardly but maintained a coldly impassive facial expression. He nodded to the guard, standing stiffly at attention near the door. The guard raised his left hand, and eight men, tightly bound and blindfolded, were brought into the room. Joseph and Barrington, the soldiers who had initially captured Obadele, were included in that line, as was their Commander.

Joshua sat at the head of the table and broke the silence. "The Omowale that escaped is a high ranking operative among the nags."

He continued, "His escape could not have been achieved without help. Only eight individuals came in contact with him. It is possible that one helped him or that all eight helped him. I don't know, and it really doesn't matter."

He paused and then continued, the tone and loudness of his voice increasing, "It has been suggested that we could measure the Pineal Extract "--he spat out the last two words contemptuously-- "and implicate those with the highest levels as traitors to the Horde."

Joshua paused again, as the men whispered among themselves. He said loudly, "This is not acceptable. There is the possibility of error, and the guilty ones would continue to betray us whenever possible. We will survive the Omowale's escape, but we cannot give the traitors among us the opportunity to do even greater damage. We must cut our losses."

He looked intently at the guard who had brought in the prisoners and nodded almost imperceptibly.

The guard acknowledged the gesture and snapped to attention. He recited loudly and rigidly, "It is never a good time to die but now is your time." He then walked behind the bound men and took the blindfolds off each of them.

After he had removed the last blindfold, he jerked to the attention posture and clicked his heels together. Immediately, eight more soldiers marched into the room as if on cue, and each stood behind one of the prisoners.

The guard then slowly said, "Your. Time. Is. Now." with long pauses between each word.

With the word, "your", each soldier pulled a large machete from a sheath at their left side. With the word "time", they held it at attention at the level of their heads. When "is" was spoken, they drew the large sharp blades back to the right. When "now" was uttered, they each decapitated the man standing in front of them.

As the severed heads fell to the floor, the headless wretches stood for several seconds before falling forward toward the Council table. The blood spurted all over the spellbound individuals sitting at the table. They were all transfixed and could not move.

Joshua smiled as the sight and odor of blood filled the room and spilled onto everyone within reach. His voice jerked the room back to reality, "I would offer you the opportunity to drink the blood, but the traitor should not poison us."

The Councillors all looked at Joshua with awe. They laughed politely at his attempted humor but were obviously petrified with fear.

John, sitting at Joshua's right hand, beamed. "Joshua is a genius," he thought. "This act will add to Joshua's legend and ensure the loyalty of the Council--no matter what happens."

Joshua excused the guards from the room and began the meeting. It was a bizarre and gory sight. Blood covered the floor and the Horde men who were sitting on the side of the massacre. The headless bodies lay closely adjacent to the long oval conference table, some still twitching, making a scratchy noise against the floor. The eyes on the severed heads were staring with horrified expressions on the faces.

"We must ensure the loyalty of the Asians. They are a courageous but pragmatic people, so we must continue to convince them that we are the future. The problem is that they have more in common with the nags. They will not respond to intimidation. In fact, attempts at intimidation would probably drive them farther from us.

One of the Councillors, Bob, was still staring at one of the twitching, headless, bloody bodies. The head, lying to his right, was turned so that the eyes stared upwards as if he was a part of the meeting. Joshua looked intently at him and asked, "Bob, do you have any suggestions?"

Bob turned slowly towards Joshua, a plastic smile framing eyes that revealed intense hatred. He said nothing.

John tried to speak, but Joshua silenced him with one gesture, holding up his hand, palm facing John while looking at Bob. Joshua spoke again, more quietly this time, a definite threat in his voice, "Bob, I asked you if you have any suggestions that would help us solve this situation." His voice was soft but dangerously insistent. The tension in the room was palpable.

Bob replied after an uncomfortable pause, in an equally soft and intense voice, "Why don't we meet with the Asian leaders who are sympathetic to us and get their input?"

John slowly exhaled in relief. He had been trying to alert Joshua that Barrington, one of the beheaded men, was Bob's younger brother, with whom Bob was very close. Bob was one of the most popular Generals in the armed forces and specialized in tactical matters. He was considered to be the most brilliant tactician in Europa and Threekay. He could be a dangerous enemy, as well as a valued ally.

Joshua looked intently at Bob. He was extremely upset at John but didn't show it. He knew that John was trying to warn him but was insulted that John actually failed to realize that he had deeply studied each of the men he executed. He was also angrily disappointed that John, himself, had left that bit of knowledge to chance.

"Well then, Bob will contact our Asian allies and set up a meeting..say within the next seven to ten days?" Joshua said, not breaking his glare at Bob.

Bob returned the glare and said softly, "It will be done. I will notify you and the Council of the day, time and place."

Joshua replied, "Good. We await the day and time, but the place will be here in this room."

"As you wish," Bob said, after a brief hesitation, still glaring at the murderer of his brother.


## The Omowales Meet

Obadele and Kofi had been reared in the same style except for one very basic difference: Nana Ade had made all his grandchildren start "from the bottom" in terms of duties, responsibility and authority. He elevated or promoted them only when they had accomplished the necessary tasks at hand. He even occasionally demoted them after severe breaches of protocol, which were rare. They all started out running simple errands, then more complex errands, then cleaning part of a room, then cleaning a whole room, then the house, then the house plus the yard, and finally keeping up those houses in their community in which men were missing due to Horde attacks or other reasons. Obadele initially had even more responsibility because, as the oldest, he was made responsible for Kwame and Aisha. Only when he consistently showed himself responsible was he allowed to start his training.

During his childhood, Obadele was allowed to play like other children, but he also had to keep up his grades in school. Although the concept of testing and grading were antiquated, they were still used but in a different context than centuries earlier.

Grades were not dependent in any way on tests. Tests were used to judge the efficacy of the teaching, not the learning. Grades were derived from the students' total performance, both objective and subjective. The subjective aspect was believed most important because it meant that the objective material learned could be used appropriately. Objective teaching alone, perfected by Horde, created unthinking, unfeeling robotic beings who memorized rotely and left creativity to chance. The minimum grade required to pass was 90%, but only if the teaching team was convinced that the student had exerted his or her best effort. If someone did their best and scored less than 90%, remedial work was provided, and the teaching team was re-evaluated. If someone scored 90% and did not do their best, they had to repeat the course.

Kofi's upbringing differed in that he was given his duties and responsibilities in a step-wise fashion regardless of his accomplishments.   He had no younger siblings to be responsible for, and this was also proved to be a glaring hole in his development.

Baba Kamau had also stressed excellence so that the differences were small, however.  Obadele's level of maturity seemed slightly greater than Kofi's. However, Kofi's natural curiosity, dedication to detail and desire to excel made his overall achievements at least as impressive as Obadele's.


## Omowale Family Gathering

The Day after the Council meeting, the Omowales gathered at Nzinga's house for dinner.  Nzinga and Jomo had decided that it was best to get them all together to stress their many commonalities. rather than to fear their differences.

Kofi and Fumi arrived first.  They only lived around the corner from Nzinga.  Before they settled in, Obadele, Amma, Kwame, Aset, and Aisha arrived.

Obadele was proud of his family. Even though all Human inhabitants of Heart felt a kinship to each other, the direct lineages were even closer.  There was even a friendly rivalry among clans to outdo each other in contributions to society as a whole. Kwame often laughingly called this "cooperative competition". The competition was never the primary goal and never prevented complete cooperation between competing clans, however.  As a result, all clans were distinguished and respected. The Omowales were, however, giants among giants.

The pre-dinner conversation was lighthearted, and they all basked in the presence of their loved ones. Fumi seemed very happy. Musicians were usually cheerful and upbeat. At dinner that night, she smiled constantly and laughed frequently. She was taller than Kofi by half a head and didn't downplay her height. She wore her short dark brown hair naturally. Her complexion was the color of the skin of a canteloupe and seemed to glow when she smiled. Fumi and Kofi had been together for fifteen years, many of which found Kofi traveling to various parts of Heart, frequently with Obadele, representing the Council of Elders. They had not become parents yet.

As they sat down to eat, Nzinga asked Kofi and Fumi to pour libation and start the Ancestors' plate. Kofi looked surprised. Although he was Obadele's senior by eighteen months, they were in the same Age-Grade. He thought that if Nzinga or Jomo didn't pour libation, Obadele would. He was honored to be asked and to be given the opportunity.

Aset and Amma hadn't known Fumi before their marriages brought them all together. They had become friends, but because of the distance between their homes in Menefer and Atlantis, they had not been as close as they would have liked. Aset had always had the feeling that they would be close whenever the opportunity presented itself. This week proved to be that opportunity.

Although slightly older, Fumi was in the same age-grade as Amma and Aset and was a pioneer in using tones and rhythms for healing. Aset, as a Healer, was fascinated by the work that Fumi had done. She had even suggested that Fumi take some training in the Healing Arts to fully understand the profound ramifications of her research. Fumi had been flattered to be invited to join such an illustrious and honorable profession by one of its brightest lights. However, she had actually stumbled upon her discoveries accidentally and had no interest in learning about the Healing Arts.

The dinner went well. No serious topics were discussed, but everyone present enjoyed the family time. Whatever uneasiness had been exposed in Council was erased and forgotten. They all left happy and secure in the knowledge that their family ties were safe.

## After Dinner

Later that night, Amma and Obadele slipped out of the hotel and walked hand in hand through the city. The night was quiet, except for the sound of the occasional passing car or bus. There were not many people out on the street. For a long time, as they walked, neither spoke. They were both experiencing a gamut of emotions. They were deliriously happy to be together again and tremendously saddened by the prospect of the threatened carnage.

After the two had walked for almost an hour, they saw a park bench across the street and headed for it. Although it was located at the edge of a park, it was out in the open. Before they had reached it, Obadele had carefully studied the surrounding area in a 360-degree circle. Amma felt the tension in his hand. She understood that because of his training as a Protector, he could rarely be totally relaxed. The fear of Horde terrorism was everpresent. She was happy that she had been able to surround him with love and peace of mind at their home. Like her mother, Amma was fascinated with the life of Protectors. She had adored her father and had been extremely close to her younger brother. She had excelled in martial arts and worked out with her husband almost every day when he wasn't traveling. Amma had learned a great deal from Obadele during these workouts.

They sat on the bench and quietly watched the scenes unfold on the street and sidewalk in front of them as if they were the audience in a reality play. When Obadele placed his arm around Amma, she laid her head on his shoulder. They still did not speak. It wasn't necessary. Words were unnecessary and probably would have been inadequate.

After what seemed like hours, Obadele spoke first. His words made Amma laugh loudly. "I'll bet Kwame and Aset have the 'Do Not Disturb' sign on their door at the hotel."

Amma laughed so hard that she couldn't speak but nodded vigorously to show that she agreed. They fell silent again. The weight of the current situation weighed heavily on them.

A group of young people approached them, talking and laughing. They were about fifteen or sixteen years of age, and there were eight of them. There were three Human boys, two Human girls, one Mulat girl, one Loyalist boy and one Loyalist girl. They were having a good time but still had the presence of mind to pause in front of the adult couple as they passed. They quietly and respectfully greeted Amma and Obadele, acknowledging their Elders. As one, they said, "Hotep" as they passed Amma and Obadele.

Obadele nodded, smiled and replied, "Shemhotep!"

The young people replied, again in unison, "Medasi" and moved on quietly. When they were about a half block away, they resumed their animated conversation and loud laughing.

Amma looked up at her man, from his shoulder and smiled.

"What?" he asked.

She smiled even more broadly and said, "You will be a wonderful father."

He kissed her lightly on the lips and replied, "Only because you will be a wonderful mother and will guide me."

They embraced, and at that moment, everything seemed right.

The walk back to Nkrumah Square was quicker. Although their arms were around each other, there was a quickness in their steps and an urgency in their movements.

When they walked into their suite, they both reached for the 'Do Not Disturb" sign to hang outside the door. When their hands met, reaching for the sign, they collapsed to the floor with laughter.

## The Next Day

A second Council meeting was scheduled for the following day. This was a working meeting and was intended to plan the strategy of Humanity against this latest threat from the Horde. Representatives from all the Nomes in New Alkebulan were expected to be present, even from Pacifica, the furthest Human outpost and perhaps the weak link in Humanity's existence and defense. Representatives from the Up South region of Atlantis and the Down North region of DuSable were already in Menefer.

The Omowales had breakfast together before the meeting. At the risk of being accused of being politicians, they wanted to see where everyone stood, whether they were together in their positions or whether they would disagree. They were careful to avoid consensus-building outside the Council Chambers and didn't try to win each other over because, in this situation, that was playing politics. There would definitely be no compromises.

## The Plan Develops

The mood of the council chamber was somber. Obadele's report had been thoroughly digested by each member. Everyone was anxious to hear what everyone else had decided the best course would be.

Jomo opened the meeting with a loud, "Agoo."

The body answered with a subdued "Amee" said in unison. After the Libation, they waited to hear what Jomo would say next.

Jomo stated in a loud, expressive voice, "Humans! We are faced with a situation that we have never faced before."

The room murmured as each person softly agreed with him and called on the Ancestors to intervene.

"What are we to do?" Jomo asked the assemblage.

There was a long silence. Nobody wanted to be the first to suggest a radical solution. Everyone in the Council realized that only a radical solution would solve the problem that they all faced.

Jomo asked, "Humans, do you trust me?"

As one, the Council erupted in a loud, "Yes!"

Jomo looked around at the faces of his friends and comrades. After a long pause, he said, "I have been presented with a plan. It is dangerous, but its success could possibly ensure decades, if not centuries, of peace on Heart. Its failure would not change the situation as it exists at this moment. The risk will be to only one person, but the potential benefit will be for all Humanity."

Soft murmurs filled the Council chambers as the assembled Humans, Mulats and Loyalists whispered among themselves.

After another pause, Jomo continued, "Friends, the reason why I asked you if you trust me is because, in order for this plan to succeed, it must be a closely held secret. I cannot discuss it with anyone who does not already know about it. I ask again, do you trust me?"

Before anyone could respond, Kofi stood and waited to be given permission to speak.

Amma and Aset held their breaths, trying not to look more knowledgeable than anyone else. They dared not look at each other.

Jomo said, "Speak, Kofi Omowale"

Kofi looked around and said, "There is no one more trusted than the Honorable Jomo. I think that I speak for the Council when I say that we will go the route that Jomo suggests in the manner that he feels best."

Kofi looked around the chamber, and almost everyone present was nodding in agreement with his pronouncement. He continued, "I would respectfully request that we be allowed to prepare other responses in case of the failure of your plan."

Jomo nodded. "That is an excellent request, Brother Kofi. We must prepare for all possible eventualities. I would suggest that you and Brother Obadele assemble a committee of your choosing and present plans to us by the end of the week."

Jomo opened the floor to other suggestions and comments. Hearing nothing, he dismissed the Council with plans to meet the following day.

## Aisha and Joshua

Later that afternoon, after hearing that the Council accepted the plan, Aisha set it in motion by calling Joshua at the private number that he had left her in numerous messages. She realized that she was treading on deadly ground. She had never met her biological father, but she felt like she knew him because her grandfather, Baba Ade, had made sure that she was familiar with him. He had even made her establish communication with her paternal grandparents, Joshua's parents. Joshua's mother had died in a Horde terrorist attack several years previously, and Joshua was probably unaware of his mother's death. Aisha had made sure that her grandfather, Moses, the old Loyalist, was cared for. She did it more out of obligation than affection, however. She didn't hate him, she just didn't really know him and felt very little for him.

She had initially rebelled against Baba Ade, not wanting to know anything about Joshua or his parents, but Ade had gently persisted, and Aisha could never refuse her grandfather. Because of this teaching and the smattering of information that she had gotten from other people, she felt like she knew Joshua fairly well. She definitely knew that he was no dummy but obviously had a weakness for her since he had never given up trying to reach her. She also realized he was trying to appeal to the Horde part of her to use her against her Human family.

He answered on the second ring with, "What?" His tone was gruff and arrogant, probably the result of the power that he held.

She hesitated briefly, and then said softly but firmly, "I don't know what to call you."

It was Joshua's turn to hesitate as he realized who had called him. He looked at the faces surrounding him and motioned for them to leave. He could not betray himself by demonstrating softness or any type of weakness. When the men looked puzzled and hesitated, he growled into the phone, "Hold on!" and then barked at the men, "Get out, now!"

When the men were all out of his office, he turned on his "checker" to find out if any eavesdropping devices were in operation. When he was satisfied that their conversation was truly private, he returned to the phone and connected the video to the wall monitor so he could get a good look at her. His heartbeat quickened. She looked so much like her mother! He hoped that his facial expression had not betrayed the turmoil of emotions that he was feeling

"To what luck of providence do I have the honor of this call," he asked, trying unsuccessfully to sound sarcastically distant and unfeeling.

Aisha heard the tenderness in his voice and saw his reaction to her image, however, and marveled. She had not thought him capable of such emotion. She said, "I want to get to know this man, Joshua. He forced a sperm donation on my mother and is responsible for me being here. I feel that I must know who or what he is." She slightly emphasized the "what" and became silent, awaiting his reply.

He didn't hesitate, "Do I have your Omowale cousin's recent visit to Europa to thank for this call? It is sooo unexpected." He drew out the "sooo" in a sarcastic manner.

"I admit that my *brother*, Obadele, did influence this call indirectly in part. I should also say to you now, that should we develop a relationship, I will not conspire with you against Humanity. I know no strategic secrets and would not reveal them if I did, so we need to get that out first."

Joshua felt defensive. He knew that his overtures to Aisha over the years had been interpreted as trying to "turn" Aisha to his way of thinking, but when confronted with the actual words, he realized again that he felt deeply for this half-human, half Horde female who was his daughter. She was his only child as far as he knew. He realized that he had to be careful to avoid letting her know just how vulnerable he was.

"Old man Ade did his work well," Joshua said, as much to himself as to Aisha.

Aisha remained silent but was buoyed by the statement.

Joshua asked, "Are you a spy?" He knew that the Humans valued the Maatic Code so much that they generally refused to lie. However, if Obadele had actually found out all that was planned, even the Humans would lie for the sake of their survival.

Aisha marveled at her father's cunning as well as his knowledge of Humanity. She had been warned by Nzinga and Jomo to expect that question or one like it.

"I do want to get to know you and try to understand you," she answered truthfully. "But if you reveal to me anything that will help my people, I will use it. You should understand that fact before we go any further with this experiment."

Her answer confirmed to Joshua that she was on a fact-finding mission. The timing of her contact was obvious. However, she had said that she wanted to get to know him, and he knew that it was true. Despite himself, he smiled into the phone and felt his heart rate quickened again. He wanted to say to her that she was also Horde, and to call Humans her "people" was inaccurate. However, he thought better of saying this because he didn't want to damage the relationship with his daughter before it even started.

"How is your mother?" he asked, trying to change the subject.

"You don't care about her," Aisha said, raising her now icy voice. "Don't you even pretend to care about her! You brutally raped her and then decapitated the love of her life in front of her. This is going to be between us. Leave her out of it or forget it.

Mixed emotions washed over Joshua. On the one hand, he really did not want to know about Adwoa, but on the other hand, he was curious as to how Adwoa was doing. He realized that he was unwilling to admit to himself that his feelings for Aisha were actually poorly submerged under his gruff exterior. He was glad that his Horde subordinates knew little of his previous relationships with the Omowales. Although he saw these feelings as a grave weakness, he was proud of the aggressiveness that Aisha showed in her response to him, however.

He tried to explain, "I was actually curious as to how Adwoa is doing but judging from your reaction, that is not a topic that we need to concern ourselves with at this point." After a brief pause, he asked, "What do you have in mind?"

Aisha smiled inwardly. This was what she wanted... to get to the point quickly. "Perhaps I can visit you eventually."

"Aren't you afraid?" He responded.

"Yes." Aisha replied truthfully, "I am, but that is the only way you and I will be able to spend time together. I know that you can't come to New Alkebulan."

"What are you afraid of?

"I have heard terrible things about you. I know of your brutality and deceptions."

"Do you think that I would harm my own daughter?"

She hesitated before answering, "Yes, I know that you would hurt me if it served your plans."

This answer stunned him. He had not realized that his reputation in New Alkebulan was so heartlessly brutal that his own daughter would be so convinced that he would harm her. Again, he had mixed feelings. He wanted to be known as a ruthless leader, but at the same time, he wanted his only child, his daughter, to feel safe with him. He was at a loss for words for the first time in years.

His hesitation alarmed Aisha initially, but she quickly realized that he was conflicted. This was good! She decided to play it out. "You couldn't have thought that I would trust you with my life completely."

"I was just surprised that you'd admit to me that you felt that way. If that's how you feel, why would you be willing to risk coming to New Europa?"

"Because I have no intention of giving you reason to suspect that I was a danger to you or to your plans."

He liked that answer. He felt she was sincere in her stated desire to get to know him better. He did remember that she had said previously that she would use any information. that she uncovered to help Humanity but was pleased that he might actually develop a relationship with his flesh and blood. "Does your mother know of this decision to get to know me?"

"No," she again answered truthfully. "She would be tremendously upset if she knew."

"Do your brothers know?"

She hesitated before answering that Obadele and Kwame were not aware of her plans. Again, Joshua felt good about her answer because he knew that the Maatic Codes prevented her from lying.

"If I decide to trust you and visit New Europa, how do I know that you or your followers won't try to keep me there against my will when I'm ready to leave? How can I be sure that you won't hold me for some ransom? How can I feel safe?"

"I don't know what I can say to answer that question. I only know that, as your father, I don't want to see you hurt in any way. As long as I'm in power in New Europa, you will be safe and free here with certain limitations."

"What limitations?"

"Of course, you will not be allowed to visit any strategic areas."

"I expected as much. We need to have several conversations, though, before I'll feel comfortable coming there."

"I understand."

"So... Call me when you feel like talking further."

He wanted to say that he was happy that she was finally coming to her senses but realized that those words could actually derail his budding relationship with the daughter he now knew that he always yearned to know. So before disconnecting, he simply said, "I will."

## The Omowales

Before the next Council meeting, The Omowales had breakfast at Kofi and Fumi's apartment. Fumi was a gracious hostess, fussing over every detail to make sure that everyone was comfortable. She appreciated the help that Amma and Aset gave her.

Kwame asked, just before they sat down to eat, "Where is Aisha?"

The women all continued doing what they were doing, trying not reveal anything. Aset looked up at Kwame, wondering what to say that would not damage the Maatic Code.

Nzinga quickly but casually answered, "She said that she had something to complete that would be a surprise. She was so secretive."

The ladies all quietly relaxed, grateful to their brilliant Elder for saving the situation.

Obadele sat down next to Amma and said, "She has always had something going on since we were children."

Nzinga poured libation, and they settled down to eat and talk.

Kofi said, "I wish that I knew what plan Jomo was talking about at the meeting. It would be so much easier to create a fall-back plan if we knew what the original plan was to be."

Obadele added, "I feel you on that. If I didn't have so much confidence in Jomo, I would have objected or at least started a discussion."

Nzinga nodded and said nothing as did the other Omowale ladies.

## The Second Conversation

Aisha was thinking about how she would gather information, knowing that her father would be watching her every move. It was a daunting task, but a necessary one if Heart was to be saved. She was surprised when the vid-phone buzzed. She looked at the message and saw that Joshua was calling. "Already," she thought.

She answered, "Greetings...I still don't know what to call you."

"Just call me Joshua," he said, thinking that if things went well, he might allow her to call him Josh in private, as her mother had once done.

"This was quick... Joshua," she said. "I didn't expect you to call me back so soon."

"I am a decisive man. Any leader has to be able to make split-second decisions. You are my daughter. We should have a relationship. You deserve to know me."

"I know your father and knew your mother, and they tried to tell me about the boy they raised."

"What do you mean, 'knew' my mother?"

"She was killed in the last offensive that you launched against us. She was shopping at a supermarket and got caught in the crossfire. She transitioned shortly after that. It's been about three years now."

That news hit Joshua like a ton of bricks. Although he had turned his back on his parents, he still felt a strange sensation of sadness in hearing about his mother's transition. He felt the need to hide these emotions from his daughter until he really got to know her.

"How is Moses?" he asked, avoiding further mention of his mother.

"He is good. He is lonely but goes to a senior citizen center where he has made a lot of friends, Human, Loyalist and Mulat." She emphasized the last part of her news because she was upset that he seemed to have no regard for his mother's demise and his participation in the cause of her death.

She then asked, "Is there any way you can guarantee my safety, other than your word?"

"I will take a Blood Oath. Other than that, I cannot."

She was relieved. Blood Oaths were perhaps the only things that Horde considered to be very sacred. "If you're willing to do that, you must have a witness that will also pledge with a blood oath to protect me and return me home, in case you are unable to."

This pleased him very much. He had toyed with the idea of trying to pair her with John Paul, and by having John take the oath with him, they would get to know each other, and maybe...

"That is agreeable. Who will you have to witness the oath...your brothers?"

"No. They will not know that I am in Europa. I will ask my ElderMother, Nzinga, to serve as my witness."

"That too is acceptable. When will this take place?"

"The sooner, the better. I have to be truthful with you, I am hoping to at least broker some type of understanding to prevent so much bloodshed."

Was she serious? Surely, she knew that Horde thrived on violence and bloodshed. Surely, she realized that Horde would never stop contesting for control of Heart. Was she that naïve or that cunning? He looked at her image on the vidscreen and decided that her decision to contact him was based in foolish wishful thinking. Like most Horde, he was extremely misogynistic and had little respect for females' intellect or wisdom, especially Human females.

She added, "I will contact you this evening or early tomorrow after I speak with her."

## Aisha and Nzinga

Later that evening, Aisha called Nzinga to report on the two conversations that she had with Joshua. Nzinga had returned from the family meal and was relaxing with Jomo.

Aisha tried not to leave any detail out, including her impressions of the things he had said and how he had said them. Nzinga needed to be able to process as much information as possible since she had known him.

After hearing all that Aisha had to say, Nzinga said, "I think that he is trying to match you up with someone there."

"Why do you think that?

"He is agreeing too easily. He must have confidence that this person he's planning to be a son-in-law can convince you to stay with him. Did he say who that would be?"

"No, he didn't."

Jomo had been quiet up to this point but felt that he needed to add an important point, "You were wise to agree with the Blood Oath, but you must word it very carefully so as to completely protect you from not only them but from anyone else who might be a threat. There should be no loopholes."

Nzinga asked, "When will all these oaths take place?"

Aisha replied, "Tomorrow early. I want to get together with the family afterwards and then leave for Europa tomorrow night."

"OK. Jomo and I will work on the oath tonight, and when you come by in the morning, we will perfect it."

## The Blood Oath

Aisha slept poorly that night and rang Nzinga's doorbell bright and early the following morning. She was surprised that Jomo answered and wondered if he had been there all night. It was not a "big deal" because they were both single, fully grown adults, although she was not aware that they had undergone any engagement or betrothal rituals. As Elders, they did not have to submit to an evaluation by other Elders for permission to marry.

Nzinga had breakfast prepared, salmon, eggs, toast, and fruit. Aisha had been thinking about her upcoming adventure so much that she had forgotten to eat. The aroma of the food caused her empty stomach to cramp.

They sat down to eat, and Jomo poured libation and served the Ancestors. Again, a surprise that he would perform these rituals in Nzinga's home. Aisha ate ravenously, so much so that Nzinga and Jomo exchanged smiling glances.

After they had eaten and Aisha helped Jomo clean up the dishes (another surprise), they settled down to discuss the document that Nzinga and Jomo had created. It read:

*"With my blood, I pledge to always protect Aisha Omowale with my life if necessary, I will not allow any harm, physical, mental, or*

*emotional, to come to her. I will not allow her to be forced to do or say anything that she does not want to do or say and will not allow anyone else to do so. I will not force her to stay in Europa or Threekay or anywhere that she does not want to be and will not allow anyone else to do so. I will not give her any food or drink or any other substance that would harm her or alter her state of mind and will prevent anyone else from doing so. I will not implant monitoring or spying devices on or in her person or in her quarters and will prevent anyone else from doing so. I will not force her to take on friends and responsibilities that she does not desire. I pledge and swear all these things with my blood and on my life."*

Aisha was impressed. This covered just about everything that she had considered. She especially liked the word "always" because there might be other occasions that the oath would be needed.

Later that morning, after Jomo had moved to another room so that he would not be seen, Aisha and Nzinga called Joshua. He answered after the third beep and gruffly greeted them, "Speak"!

Nzinga scolded him, "Joshua! Have you forgotten your manners, or have you lost your mind? You know that you don't greet your Elders in that manner!"

Joshua was glad that John had not yet arrived to hear this disrespect from a Human. He also realized that she was right. She had been one of his favorite teachers and was responsible for him being taught mannerly protocol. He had actually liked and respected her and enjoyed being in her classroom.

"I am not under your thumb anymore, old lady. I am a leader. You should not speak to me in your present tone," he replied.

"No matter who or what you are, you should respect your Elders!" Nzinga retorted. She did realize that Horde culture worshipped youth and youthfulness and hated the fact of their inevitable aging. She was trying to gauge how far the quiet boy she had taught had slipped into the inferno of Horde Culture.

After a pause, Joshua said quietly, "We are not accomplishing anything now. Let's get to the business that we came for. I hear my witness coming in now."

John Paul entered the chamber, apologizing for his tardiness but stopped talking when he felt and saw the glare from Joshua.

Joshua made the introductions, "Nzinga and Aisha, this is my second-in-command, John Paul, the leader of ThreeKay. John Paul, this is Nzinga, the mother of Amma Omowale and this," he said softly, "is Aisha Omowale, my daughter."

John Paul struggled to maintain calm. He had heard rumors that Joshua fathered a child with a Human. John Paul knew of the rape of the Buah woman but hadn't known for sure if a child was conceived. He looked at Aisha closely. She was actually beautiful! She was tall and looked nothing like her father except that she had his flashing eyes. She had a mocha complexion, and her body was voluptuous. He felt a familiar stirring in his loins, just looking at her.

Joshua's daughter! A Mulat! Even though Joshua had not told him why they were there, he began to suspect something very devious.

Joshua looked into John's eyes and said, "Aisha is to come to visit us tomorrow for as long as she chooses, and I need a witness and a co-signer of a Blood Oath to guarantee her safety. I'm sure you won't mind."

To say that John was shocked would have been a gross understatement. He was both honored and wary. He was honored that Joshua would trust him to protect his only daughter. He was wary because of how the other members of the Council might see this arrangement. John was ambitious and intended to take Joshua's place at the head of the Council eventually and did not want to ruin his chances. He decided to agree to the Blood Oath because of his great respect for Joshua and for the lessons that he would learn over the next few weeks.

"I would be honored, Joshua! Hello Nzinga and Aisha."

"Hotep, John Paul," Nzinga and Aisha said in unison. They both realized the paradox, however, because Horde abhorred peace.

"Well, what is the oath that you have suggested for us to take. Read it to me," Joshua demanded.

Nzinga started to request a "please" from Joshua but thought better of it. She did not want to push him into a corner where he would either lose face in front of John, who she recognized as the leader of ThreeKay or be forced to brashly negate everything that they had planned so carefully.

Aisha read the oath slowly. Joshua looked at John Paul. This was what he had expected, and he hoped that John would agree.

John returned Joshua's look and found it difficult to read. He decided to try to wait for Joshua to react. However, Joshua asked him, "What do you think, John?"

John replied, "If that is acceptable to you, it is most certainly acceptable to me."

Joshua smiled inwardly and thought, "Thatta boy, John."

Joshua pulled an ornately decorated dagger from the sheath that was hidden under his flowing overshirt and placed it on the desk. He reached under the desk and placed a bowl with a candle attached underneath next to the dagger. Then he and John positioned their left hands side by side over the bowl, and Joshua cut the palms of their hands with the dagger. They held their bleeding hands over the bowl until the bleeding stopped and the blood contained their mixed blood. After placing the dagger back on the desk, Joshua took out two large cloths, and they closed their cut fists over the cloth. Joshua reached under the desk again and brought out a firestick with which he lit the candle under the bowl. They silently waited for the blood to completely disappear.

Watching this ceremony on the wall screen made Aisha uneasy. She only then realized the full danger of what she was undertaking. She realized that she could "back out" at any time and that Nzinga would support her decision but felt that she was past the point of no return. She looked at Nzinga, who seemed transfixed on the screen.

When the blood had fully cooked, the men touched their hands together and addressed the ladies, "It is done. When should we expect you, daughter?"

Aisha felt surprised that Joshua had called her daughter but replied, "Tomorrow at midnight at the Sky border." She chose the Sky Border rather than the alleyway that Obadele. had used. The Horde needed not to be made aware of that entrance.

"We will be there."

The screen went dark.

Jomo came back into the room and said, "That went smoothly."

Nzinga mused," Joshua wants to hook you up with that John Paul person."

Aisha agreed. "I felt that too. We'll see how it develops. Perhaps he will be useful."

"Do not underestimate John Paul. He didn't get to be the leader of Threekay by being a dummy," Jomo warned. "And he already has at least two wives."

"Well, I'd have to be his number one wife," Aisha teased.

"We're getting silly now," Nzinga said, adding impishly with a sparkle in her eyes, "I guess it's time to start getting ready for the family meal this evening. Jomo, you know you're invited. I guess we can tell Aisha the secret that we will reveal tonight."

"What secret?"

"We are engaged!" Jomo beamed!

"Congratulations!" Aisha shouted. "I suspected that something was different. I am delighted!!!

They all embraced. Aisha went home to prepare for the family dinner. She also wanted to pour Libation to her father and grandfather so that they would watch over her during her upcoming "adventure". When the door closed behind Aisha, Jomo and Nzinga smiled at each other and wordlessly started cooking the feast.

## The Last Supper

Kofi and Fumi were the first to arrive, wearing matching purple outfits. They paused to remove their shoes, and by the time they had settled in the dining room, Obadele, Amma, Kwame and Aset knocked at the door.

"Agoo!" They said together.

"Amee," Jomo answered, opening the door. He returned to the kitchen to help Nzinga.

Obadele and Amma came into the foyer of the house, looking at each other quizzically while removing their shoes. Jomo seemed unusually at home, answering the door.

Amma and Aset went into the kitchen and started helping Nzinga, much like they did when they were little girls growing up. Fumi joined them, and Jomo got the hint and came out to the dining area to join the men.

"Mama, what is going on with you and Jomo? Something is going on. I can feel it in my bones."

Aset giggled at her friend's use of the old saying. Fumi smiled but didn't quite understand what was happening.

Nzinga stopped what she was doing and explained to Fumi, "Centuries ago, there was a common disease called arthritis that caused pain in the joints. Some people believed that they could forecast the weather by the degree of pain or discomfort they felt. They used that term. It later became used to forecast other events."

"I see," Fumi said, realizing that this was an "inside joke" that the other ladies had enjoyed for many years. She appreciated the explanation and the attempt to include her.

Nzinga continued peeling the cucumbers and said, without looking up, "Be patient dear, what's in the dark always comes to light."

The knock on the door filled the silence after Nzinga had quietly and gently cut off the conversation. They heard Aisha loudly say, "Agoo!!."

Again, Jomo answered the door and let Aisha come in.

During the meal, the conversation was lighthearted and flowed easily. This belied the fact of the impending chaos threatening their existence. They each attempted to avoid that conversation and just enjoy each other's company.

Finally, at the end of the meal, Nzinga, sitting at the back end of the round table, stood up. Jomo also stood and moved to stand beside her. "We have an announcement," Nzinga said. They linked their hands together and said in unison, "We are engaged."

Amma gasped. There was immediate silence in the spacious room.

"Well, somebody say something," Nzinga said.

Aset exclaimed, "That's wonderful, Nzinga!! Congratulations to you both."

Amma got up and went to the couple and embraced them. "I am sooo very happy for you."

Fumi and Aset joined the embrace while the men sat and watched. Aisha didn't move, but her smile lit up the room.

Kofi asked, "Just when will this blessed event take place? There is so much going on."

Fumi turned to her husband and said softly, "Hush, my beloved. Don't destroy this magical moment."

Kofi apologized to everyone, explaining that it was not his intent to disrespect or negate the moment. He started to add that he was concerned with the Horde offensive but thought that it was better left unsaid.


## The Crossing

That night, after hiding her small copter in the brush at the gate called the Sky Border, Aisha waited patiently as the

Human guards changed shifts. She hoped that the Horde guards had been alerted to her passing through by Joshua and posed no threat to her. The Sky Border was a narrow passage that held very little strategic advantage for either side. The terrain on both sides of the border was rugged with mountains and valleys that made it difficult to move vehicles, heavy equipment, and large groups of men. The air was equally difficult to use strategically.

She had informed one guard, a Mulat woman, her age-grade sister from Atlantis, named Bisa, who would provide a way for her to cross without being detected. Shortly after midnight, Bisa gave the signal, and Aisha quietly slipped through the partially open gate. Bisa had disabled the alarm but had stressed that she could leave it disabled for no longer than thirty seconds, so the timing had to be perfect.

When Aisha stepped through the gate, a gruff voice said, "Put your hands up and move forward slowly."

She did as she was told and, after three steps, felt rough hands feeling all over her body. Before she could react, a new voice asked in a commanding voice, "What the hell are you doing, Reuben?"

The rude guard, Reuben, a burly man with sandy light brown hair and steel gray eyes, said without looking up, "Just getting ready to have some fun with this half-breed."

He looked up and saw John Paul glaring at him. He instantly recoiled and almost fell. He stiffly jumped to attention and said, "Leader John, I wasn't expecting you to be here."

John stepped up to the larger man and asked," Did you not get orders stating that this woman was to be treated with the utmost respect?"

"Yes, but…"

"Did you feel that those orders were so trivial that. you didn't have to obey them?"

"No, sir, but…"

"Well then, why were you groping her? That is not a show of respect!"

"I'm sorry, sir," Reuben groveled.

"Yes. You are sorry, but not as sorry as you will be."

After voicing the threat, John Paul turned to Aisha and asked, "Are you alright Aisha?"

She assured him that she was fine, and he proceeded to welcome her to New Europa. He made an effort to be as charming as he knew how. Seeing Aisha in person for the first time, he was almost in awe of her beauty. He almost forgot that she was very dangerous.

"I apologize for the rudeness of that welcome, Sister Aisha," he pandered. This ignorant buffoon will be punished, I promise."

Aisha stood to her full height and said, "I would expect it." She knew that this statement would impress not only John Paul but also Reuben and that this exchange would be repeated throughout New Europa eventually.

Hearing this, Reuben became terrified. He didn't know who this woman was, but she must have been especially important for John Paul to personally greet her. And because of his behavior, he knew that a painful punishment awaited him. He decided to appeal to his former commanding officer for help.

### Aisha and Joshua

John beckoned to Aisha to follow him and started walking the fifty yards through the grass towards his copter. He was extremely impressed by her beauty and of the way that she responded after Reuben's ham-handed affronts, and if Joshua's plans were successful, she would be his wife. Because of who she was, however, she would have to be his chief wife. His current chief wife, Lorna, would not like this, but that didn't matter, and he could control her.

Aisha remained quiet during the walk. Her training had kicked in, and her senses were heightened when Reuben had touched her. John Paul may have saved Reuben from being seriously injured because her martial arts training had her ready to hurt him badly. As they walked, she continued to be vigilant but sensed that the immediate danger had passed. She concentrated on John Paul. Nzinga had warned her that Joshua had at least one ulterior motive, to get her married. Was it to John Paul? She decided to start her fact-finding.

When they were in the copter, and the course had been input, she asked John Paul, "So, tell me about you, John."

He smiled inwardly. This was a good sign. Aisha was actually interested in finding out about him...or was she just prying to get information? He decided to go along with her to see where it would lead.

"Well, I'm from ThreeKay, and I am your father's second-in-command. And, as you know, I took the Blood Oath to protect you. I am loyal to Joshua, he is not only a great leader, but he is also a brilliant man."

"I suppose that I can appreciate your loyalty, but what are your goals and aspirations? Are you married? Do you have children?"

"You are certainly not shy in asking these questions. My instincts tell me to ask why you want to know, but I will answer. My goal is to follow your father until he retires, and my aspiration is to become the next leader of *our* people." He emphasized "our" in "our people. He hesitated and added, "I do not wish to overthrow him or engineer a coup. To answer your other question, I have three wives and seven children.

Aisha then asked, "Is my father married? Do I have siblings?"

"He is not married," John Paul answered proudly, "but he does not lack female companionship. He has as many as twelve consorts. To my knowledge, you are his only child."

"I see," Aisha said, lapsing into silence again.

After a few more minutes, John asked Aisha, "Tell me about you. Are you married? Do you have children? Why are you here? "

Aisha turned towards John Paul, who was staring at her and smiled at him, "You aren't shy either. I am not married and have no children. Why I am here is more complicated. I want to get to know the man who forced his sperm into my mother, and I want to try to broker some kind of peaceful understanding between Humans and Horde."

He didn't respond, and again, silence filled the copter for the remainder of the journey. Aisha tried to doze off to sleep but was too anxious and hypervigilant to sleep.

Two hours later, the copter landed in the dark at the entrance to a domed estate. The palatial house and huge yard were completely enclosed by the transparent dome. A swimming pool, tennis court and basketball court were also enclosed. The entire estate was surrounded inside and outside the dome by a tall, eighteen-foot fence topped with barbed wire. The estate could only be seen from the air. Two huge albino men approached the copter from both sides. Aisha also noted two more men approaching the copter from the rear.

"What is your business here," demanded the albino on John's side as he approached the copter with his weapon drawn and pointed at John. When he was close enough to recognize John, he lowered his weapon and greeted him with, "Hi there, Brother John Paul." He then signaled to another man inside the dome, and an opening appeared just above where they had landed.

Without a word, the copter elevated, and John guided it through the opening and approached the house. From a distance, Aisha could make out the outline of a man on the wrap-around porch. When they landed in front of the porch next to three other copters, Joshua opened Aisha's door.

"Welcome home, daughter," he said.

"Thank you for the welcome, but I must remind you that this is not my home," Aisha retorted, ignoring Joshua's proffered hand and getting out of the copter without his help.

"I hope that you will come to consider this to be at least your second home," Joshua said, stepping back. "Please come in. Do you have luggage?"

"No. I didn't want to arouse suspicion by carrying luggage. I knew that I could get clothing here."

"I see that you're smart as well as beautiful. You look so much like your mother. How is she?"

"I thought that I had made it clear that she is not to be discussed. I can leave now if you can't abide by that condition."

"My bad," Joshua said, "it won't happen again. Please come in. Victoria will show you to your quarters and will be available to care for your every need."

He clapped his hand twice and a Horde woman, slender, brunette and no older than nineteen or twenty years seemed to appear from the shadows. She was not as tall as Aisha and assumed a subservient posture. She bowed from her waist and said, "This way, Mistress."

Aisha stopped and looked at the woman. Victoria looked downwards until Aisha said, "Look at me!"

Victoria reluctantly made eye contact with Aisha, fearing that she had somehow already displeased her.

"I am not your mistress. I am not superior to you. You do not have to fear me. Call me, Aisha."

Victoria shot side glances at Joshua, looking for his reaction. He nodded his head and said, "You have heard your orders, move along now."

Aisha added, "Correction, Joshua. Those were requests, not orders. Let's go, Victoria."

"Yes, mistr-, oh, I mean, Aisha."

Aisha followed the bewildered girl into the door, which opened into a huge room with loud, gaudy colored furniture. She followed her down a hall to their left and entered a room at the end of the hall. The room was spacious and contained a king-sized canopy bed. There was a single window to the left of the bed, a large video screen adjacent to the door they had just entered, a desk and chair next to the bed with the chair facing the screen and a large sofa against the right wall. The room was painted pink, and the furnishings and bedclothes were all pink or purple.

Victoria said, "I will have a selection of dresses made available for your inspection whenever you desire."

"No, I prefer pants for the time being." Aisha had never been a girly girl and always preferred feminized masculine clothing. She had found that dresses prevented her from keeping up with her brothers and Kofi growing up.

"As you wish. When would you like to see them?"

"The sooner, the better." Aisha had no desire to stay in New Europa any longer than she had to.

She sat on the sofa and watched the girl start to leave the room. Victoria paused at the door. Looking out and around the door, she came back into the room and said, "Ms. Aisha, may I ask you a question?"

Aisha answered, "Only if you call me Aisha. Not mistress and not Ms. Aisha."

"That will be difficult, but I will try...Aisha. I have never heard anyone speak to Joshua in that way. Who are you?"

"If he hasn't let it be known, we will have to wait until he feels that the time is right to introduce me."

"Of course...Aisha. Thank you."

Victoria left the room but returned shortly with an older Horde lady rolling a rack with several dozen outfits. She also had toiletries and personal items for Aisha and placed these into the large bathroom. Aisha followed her into the bathroom and marveled at the opulence. In the bathroom, there was a solid gold toilet seat, a large shower stall and a huge gold bathtub that was also a jacuzzi. A two-sink cabinet was situated between the tub and the shower. All the fixtures were gold.

Aisha instructed the ladies to leave all the clothes for her to choose from. When they left, she settled on the sofa, wondering how she would contact Nzinga and Jomo. She had dared not bring a vid-phone. Lost in her thoughts, a soft knock at the door startled her.

"Come in," she said.

Joshua came in with a vid-phone. "I thought that you might want to let Nzinga know that you arrived safely, and I noticed that you did not bring a communication device."

He added, "This is for your use while you are here, "handing the phone to her. "It is not 'bugged,' and your conversations will be completely private and secure as we agreed. Get some rest. We have a busy day tomorrow. I want to introduce you to my Council."

Aisha thanked him and lay across the bed when he left. She fell asleep quickly.

The next morning Aisha was awakened with soft music and a knock at the door. Victoria entered with a tray of various fruit, cheese, bread, and several juices. She placed the tray on the desk and waited for instructions.

"Thank you, Victoria, that will be all for now."

Victoria started to bow but caught herself. She said, "I will be outside your door if you need anything."

Aisha ate ravenously after dedicating the Ancestral plate. "I guess I was hungrier than I thought," she mused. After showering and performing her morning rituals, including the libations to her father and grandfather, she chose a black jumpsuit. It was a bit tighter than she preferred but didn't hamper her movements. She wasn't sure what the day had in store for her, but she wanted to be ready for anything, just in case... Besides, she noted that most of the women she had seen so far wore tight clothing.

Victoria was waiting just outside her door as she had promised and walked several steps behind her as they walked to the front entrance of the house. Joshua waited for her in the foyer and looked her up and down, appreciatively, "You are indeed a beautiful woman. I did pretty good, huh?"

Aisha ignored him, turned to Victoria, and asked, "Will you be coming with us?"

Victoria glanced furtively at Joshua and said, "No, mistress. I will be here when you return."

Aisha decided not to remind Victoria about calling her mistress. Joshua must have said something to her.

"So...what do you have planned for me today, Joshua?"

"I thought that I'd take you on a tour of New Europa this morning, and we will meet with the Council this afternoon. We can rest afterwards unless there is something else that you'd like to do."

They walked outside, and Aisha was surprised to see Reuben open the door to the back of a large armored copter with several obvious laser cannons attached. He was very humble and avoided eye contact with either Aisha or Joshua. He also sported two "black eyes" and his face was bruised and swollen. John Paul stood next to Reuben and the copter.

"Good morning Joshua and a very good morning, Aisha. I hope that you rested well," he asked smiling broadly at Aisha.

Joshua mumbled in response and entered the copter. Aisha paused and returned the greeting, adding that she had indeed rested well. She entered the copter and sat next to her father. She was surprised to see that the floor of the copter was made of a transparent glass-like substance, and she could see the ground.

Joshua noted her reaction and said, "We don't like surprises. If I come under attack from the ground while airborne, it helps to see where the attack is coming from. That way, we can return fire at a target instead of shooting blindly"

Aisha felt an immense sadness. Living life with this type of paranoia was indeed preventative in attaining Wholeness. The attacks that Joshua referred to were from other Horde factions in their never-ending quest for dominance through coup after coup. She realized that Joshua really could never fully relax or trust anyone completely and that for the same reasons, he could not be trusted. She actually felt sorry for these people until she remembered that they were the reasons that Humanity had to remain so vigilant. And that vigilance was also helping to hinder Humanity's quest for Wholeness.

As they toured the countryside and the city of Nouveaux Berlin, Aisha was surprised that the degree of development exceeded her expectations. The outsides of the many tall buildings were modern and well kept, and the landscaping was excellent. She also realized that they were not constantly under attack from Humanity so that they could use their resources for reasons other than defense. A large portion of the energy and riches of Humanity was spent rebuilding after the Horde attacks. By keeping Humanity on the defense, the Horde was able to slow down the development of Wholeness.

Joshua, because of spending his formative years in New Alkebulan, and specifically in Atlantis with the Omowales, was well aware of this fact. He, more than any Horde leader, understood the potential power of Wholeness and he had used this knowledge to rise through the ranks as well as achieve and hang on to leadership. In fact, Joshua had lasted in power longer than any Horde leader in history.

### The Omowales

The morning after the family meal, Amma, Fumi and Aset decided to shop for gifts for Nzinga and Jomo. They went to vendor after vendor but could not find anything that they felt appropriate for their beloved Elders.

"I wish Aisha could help us with this. She would have some excellent ideas," Aset lamented.

"I wonder how she is doing," Fumi said, "I wasn't able to sleep last night worrying about her."

Amma replied," Joshua and John Paul took Blood Oaths to protect her. Those Blood Oaths are the only thing that Horde hold sacred. I feel better about her safety because of those oaths. My worry is that she might get caught up in the middle of one of their endless coups."

"I hadn't thought of that," Aset added. "You're right."

"Thanks for giving me something else to worry about," Fumi deadpanned.

They all laughed joylessly.


### Aisha and The Horde Council

After the tour, they landed at the capital complex, where Joshua's office chambers were located. John Paul was waiting outside with a small detachment of eight men.

"Why didn't John Paul come with us?" Aisha asked.

"We never travel together," Joshua answered. "If something were to happen to me, he must be safe, and vice versa."

Again, Aisha felt a flash of sadness at having to live life with this degree of paranoia and vigilance as she allowed herself to take John's proffered hand, stepping down from the copter. John felt a surge of expectancy that she allowed him to help her. Was she warming up to him so soon?

Observing this, Joshua again had mixed feelings. Aisha had not allowed him to help her out of the copter the previous night when she arrived but did allow John Paul to help now. At once, he was jealous and also encouraged that his plan was working.

After Joshua had disembarked, they walked to the Council chambers surrounded by the detail of guards. The room was already occupied, and the only empty seats at the huge conference table were three chairs at the head of the table. Joshua took the center seat while John Paul and Aisha took seats on either side of him.

A very pale blonde, blue-eyed man demanded from the middle of the right side of the table, "Who the hell is this half breed Nag that you force in our presence?"

Joshua calmly and casually looked at the speaker and replied in a voice so soft that even Aisha, sitting right next to him, had to strain to hear his words. "This is Aisha Omowale." He paused for a full minute. "My daughter."

There was momentary verbal bedlam in the room. Everyone who was present seemed shocked at the revelation. Everyone, John Paul, and Joshua noted, except General Bob. Aisha also noted Bob's flat affect in the face of the emotion around him. She wasn't sure of the significance, however.

Joshua raised his hand for silence, and the room became deathly quiet.

"My daughter is visiting me, and I have taken a Blood Oath along with another trusted patriot for her protection. Although he is in this room, I will not reveal his identity."

Bob said, "Of course, it is obvious that John Paul is the other."

John smiled at Joshua's tactic and said, "I am not the one. I don't know who was chosen, but I am loyal to Joshua as we all are." As he spoke the last sentence, he made a show of looking intently at Bob. He also decided to find out how Bob knew about Aisha before anyone else.

The events that she was witnessing further confirmed to Aisha that the Horde must somehow be neutralized. It was all she could do to avoid making the sign of Ka after hearing such blatant lies spoken so earnestly.

Joshua added, "The purpose of this meeting was to introduce Aisha to you, my beloved and trusted counselors so that when you see her, you, also, can also provide for her comfort and safety. We will have no business discussions in her presence, so we are now adjourned for the next fortnight."

Aisha felt relief at hearing that there would probably not be an attack for at least two weeks. She also noted that Joshua had some obvious enemies around him.

## Bob

"Reuben was right," Bob thought to himself. "This half breed girl is special to Joshua. As the book says, 'An eye for an eye and a tooth for a tooth.' She must die. I will avenge Barrington."

## Aisha and Bob

The next day, Joshua and Aisha went walking through the city with two of his bodyguard escorts. Aisha was actually getting to be more comfortable with this man. Joshua was bragging about how efficiently his government operated when as they approached an alley, a familiar figure stepped out and started walking towards them. Aisha thought *"That's Reuben"*. She looked back and saw two other men following them, and across the street, another man was watching them. Before she could say anything, the zings of several laser guns rang out, and their escorts pitched forward. Her training came to her as a reflexive reaction, and she started to stand in front of Joshua to protect him, but he had already stepped in front of her. He pulled a laser gun from his robe and shot the man across the street. She heard other weapon fire as she wheeled around to face the men following them and saw them pitch forward. Behind them, she saw John Paul jogging towards them with another man, their guns drawn.

She remembered Reuben, but he had disappeared.

As if by a signal, a copter swooped down and landed in front of them. Joshua grabbed Aisha's hand and pushed her into the copter, stumbling in after her. As it took off, she looked down through the transparent floor and saw John Paul and five other men running around, probably searching for Reuben.

"Are you alright?" Joshua asked.

"Yes," Aisha answered, "are you?"

"I'll be ok. I'm just pissed! That dammed Bob is so predictable. And to think that he was my top general."

Aisha looked at him carefully and saw that he was wounded and was losing blood rapidly from his right side. She quickly took her scarf, pressed the bleeding site and yelled at the copter pilot, "Go to the nearest hospital!! Now!!"

The pilot calmly informed her that there were hospital facilities at Joshua's home, and there was a team of Healers awaiting them.

She realized that instead of this being a trap for Joshua, it was a trap engineered by Joshua and John Paul to flush out dissidents, and she was the bait.

When they got back to Joshua's estate, there were hundreds of men surrounding the grounds and another identical copter coming in from another direction. As they landed, a team of white-clad Healers rushed to the copter and bundled Joshua into the house.

John Paul approached Aisha from the other copter and asked, "Are you alright, Aisha?"

"Yes," she answered and asked him, "What was that about?" As she asked, she saw over his shoulder that Reuben and another man were bound, blindfolded, and being taken into the house.

"Just some disgruntled officials," he deadpanned. "Would you like to observe the interrogation?"

Aisha's first instinct was to decline. She had heard about the brutality of the Horde and certainly didn't want to witness it. However, she remembered her mission and realized that she might discover some important information in the process and agreed to observe.

"I want to make sure that Joshua is alright first."

"Understandable and admirable," John Paul said, reevaluating this beautiful Mulat who had been reared by Humans. Maybe she really did care for Joshua. Did that mean that he had a chance to make her his chief wife?

As they walked into the house, he led her to the hospital wing. They were stopped at a set of black double doors by the same wrinkled old red-haired woman, Jocasta, who had brought her clothes. "Joshua is in surgery now. You should come back in three or more hours."

John nodded and beckoned for Aisha to follow him. He led her into another wing of the mansion that was obscured by a bookcase. They walked down a long, dimly lit hallway into a large room that was empty except for two naked men who were bound and gagged in chairs bolted to the floor and located in the exact center of the room. A small stool was placed in front of each of the chairs. On the far wall, there was an open floor-to-ceiling cabinet about two meters wide that contained many strange utensils.

Reuben was one of the men bound in the chair, and the other man was the one who didn't seem surprised when she was introduced to the Council. She remembered that his name was Bob.

John started laughing as they entered the room. He closed the door behind them and went to the open cabinet, reached in, and brought out an instrument that looked like a large pair of pliers. He said, "Our guest will have the pleasure of watching the animals who tried to kill her suffer."

Aisha felt sick to her stomach. None of the training that she had received from her grandfather and other teachers had prepared her for what she was about to witness.

John stepped to Reuben and ripped the gag out of his mouth and punched him in the nose, causing a bloody mess. Reuben gasped and started crying and begging for his life. Before John Paul actually touched him again, he exposed the plot and implicated General Bob as the mastermind. He claimed that he was coerced because of threats to his family.

John Paul slowly sat on the stool in front of Reuben and stared while the bawling man begged. He had an eerie and frightening (to Aisha) smile on his face. "What else, traitor?" he asked.

Reuben became quiet and asked, "What do you mean, Leader John Paul?"

"Who else was involved in the plot? We have identified the other attackers, your friends who didn't survive and are currently rounding up their families and yours. You say that you participated only because your family was threatened. So, now you may have an opportunity to save them. Just tell me who all the plotters are."

"I don't know. I was just told to kill the girl. I guess the others were supposed to kill Joshua. I thought that I'd be acting alone. I swear."

John Paul laughed incredulously, "Man, you are stupider than you look if you expect me to believe that bullshit!"

Aisha listened intently. She felt that Reuben was telling the truth. Basic tactical training taught that the less that any individual knew, the safer the plan and the planners.

"It was you that tipped Bob off to our arrival, wasn't it?"

"Yes, Leader John Paul, but...."

John Paul replaced the gag in Reuben's mouth before he could finish the sentence and ripped the gag from Bob's mouth. "OK, Mr. General, your turn. Your eyes have been popping out, so now is your opportunity to talk. Many people's futures hang on what you say to me now."

Bob said defiantly, "You will not live to see the next sunrise, asshole."

The smile on John Paul's face widened. "Dead men don't kill. You should know that all your friends and confidants and all your family members are in custody, including that foxy young wife of yours and that cute little daughter. Your young son is also being watched closely by the rearguard if you know what I mean. So, you have a great chance to improve their chances of safety and survival. You can also influence how quickly you will die."

Bob said, "You don't know who else is with me. You will spend the rest of your life watching your back."

John again smiled broadly, "You have been under surveillance since we executed Barrington for being stupid and careless. Everyone that you communicated with since then is now incarcerated and beginning their interrogation. I have saved your wife's questioning for me personally."

Immediately after speaking those words, John Paul regretted saying them in front of Aisha. He wondered how he could clean up the obvious picture that he had just painted but decided that if she were to become his wife, she should know who he is and what he is capable of doing.

"I have spoken to hundreds of people since you and Joshua murdered my brother. You can't kill them all."

"Actually, we can, and we will. It is time for a purge anyway."

"You wouldn't dare."

John beckoned to the closed door, and it immediately opened. A small man rolled in a large screen that was at least three meters in diameter. When the screen was positioned in front of the men, it came on, as if by magic. The picture revealed a room with more than a dozen people sitting in chairs facing the camera. Both Reuben and Bob's eyes popped as they recognized close friends and family in that audience.

As they watched, a laser beam swung back and forth until all the people were slumped over, dead.

John Paul's smile had not left him. "That is just the beginning. Tell me what I want to know."

Bob said, "If you really knew what you say, you know, you wouldn't be sweating us with these questions."

John Paul replied with a smirk, "Oh, but we do. Believe me, I am trying to prevent as much bloodshed as possible."

"Screw you!"

John grasped one of Bob's testicles with the pliers, and Bob screamed loudly.

At this point, Aisha had seen enough. The wanton disregard for life and callous infliction of pain and suffering was too much for her.

"I'm going to check on Joshua," she said.

"But the fun is just beginning," John Paul pleaded. "There's more to come."

"I'll pass." Aisha left the room and returned to the hospital wing. Jocasta was still guarding the door, but Aisha demanded, "How is he? I want to see him!"

The old crone replied, "They just finished the surgery, and he's in recovery. He did well and should be back to 100% in five or six weeks, but he needs his rest now".

After staring down the old lady, Aisha realized that she would be unable to see Joshua until Jocasta or John Paul permitted it, and John Paul would probably be busy for the next few hours.

"I gotta get home before the ca-ca hits the fan," she thought, "but how? Who can I trust?"

She walked back to her quarters and was joined silently by Victoria. When they entered the room, Victoria whispered,

"You must leave Aisha. I don't think that it's safe here for you." She handed Aisha a vid-phone and left the room.

Aisha immediately called Bisa, "I need to get back home immediately."

Bisa replied, "Speak to the person who gave you the vid phone. She or he can get you to the Sky Border tonight, and I'll do the rest. You should arrive no earlier than midnight."

The connection was ended, and Victoria came back into the room. "I am a Loyalist but have been unable to escape. I don't want to leave my family here, but if I help you return to New Alkebulan, I will not be able to stay here. Will you give me protection there?"

Aisha thought about it. Joshua and John Paul were just devious enough to have planned this, and Victoria might be a spy. On the other hand, she was quite correct that her life would be in danger should she aid in Aisha's escape and stay in New Europa. She realized that she had no choice. She was certain that John Paul would stall and delay her leaving, despite the Blood Oath especially considering the way he had been looking at her. His lust was palpable.

"I will protect you. I need to get to the Sky Gate shortly after, not before midnight tonight."

"I will make the arrangements. Wait here."

## The Escape

That night at about 8:00, Victoria knocked softly on Aisha's door. When she entered, she was wearing a small backpack. Aisha thought, "She can't bring that to Alkebulan. There is no telling what that is. I will take it from her just before we pass through."

They crept out of the house and walked to the entrance portal, where they entered a small two-seater copter. Victoria said, "Hide yourself under those clothes behind the seats. I frequently take Joshua's discarded clothes to my relatives so the guards should not be suspicious."

As they lifted off, a beam of light followed the copter until it reached the portal.

The guard asked, "Hey there, Vickie, where you going?"

"I'm taking these rags to my father and brothers. I'll be back in a coupla hours, Bernie. How are you doing?"

"I'd be doing much better if you gave me a chance to hang out with you some night," Bernie flirted.

"Let's talk about it when I get back. I have all night tonight off."

"Well then, hurry back," Bernie said, smiling brightly while opening the portal, "See you then."

Victoria winked, "Can't wait, stud."

When they were a safe distance from the compound, Victoria told Aisha that it was safe to sit in the passenger seat. They chatted for the remainder of the trip, which took more than three hours since Victoria's small copter was not capable of reaching the speed that John Paul's copter had reached. While they chatted, Aisha tried to evaluate whether this young woman represented a threat. If she was a spy, she was very convincing to be so young. She remembered that Horde were devilishly deceptive and could not really be sure of Victoria's motives. If she was not a spy for the Horde, she could potentially be extremely helpful to Humanity

They arrived at the Sky Gate about ten minutes before midnight and landed the copter just beyond the gate, out of visual range.

"We have a few minutes before midnight. What will we do to pass the time?" Victoria asked.

"I want you to take a Blood Oath that you are not a spy and that you do not mean New Alkebulan or the people of New Alkebulan any harm," Aisha thought but decided to wait until they were on the other side of the border to make that request.

"We can just talk. What do you want to do when we cross the Sky Gate? Do you have any skills? Would you want to attend school? What do you have in your backpack? Are you willing to take Pex?"

Victoria was surprised by this last question. "I really hadn't thought about it before. I guess that I might be inclined to try to fit in, and if Pex helps me to fit in better, then, yes, I'd be willing to take it. What I have in my backpack are pictures of my family and some papers that I found in Joshua's office. I don't know what they are but hopefully you Humans can use them to help end all the violence."

Aisha was relieved to hear this. "Good. I guess we'd better start walking to the gate."

On the other side of the border, Bisa had walked boldly to the gate and called out, "I need a real man."

The Horde guard was wary and approached the gate, looking around for a trap.

Bisa said, "There's nobody over here but me. I'm not sure that anyone will be here until the shifts change, and that will be several hours from now. What do you want to do until then to make this time interesting? What's your name anyway?

Still wary, the guard said, "I'm Arthur, and who are you? Come out of the shadows so that I can see you."

Bisa stepped closer to the gate, licked her lips, and said, "Arthur, you look simply delicious."

Arthur stared at the lovely Mulat and thought, "Normally, I'm not attracted to Nags or Mulats, but she is very good-looking and is threatening me with a good time. It will be a fun way to pass the time. Maybe she has friends that can join us later."

He said, "You have to come to this side. I'm not crossing over there."

"That would be just fine," she said seductively, "I ain't scurred of you."

As he opened the gate, she stepped across and stepped behind him as he closed it. She touched his neck with a stun rod, rendering him unconscious. As he fell, she saw movement in the shadows behind them and exhaled in relief when she saw that it was Aisha. She had a Horde girl with her.

"Welcome home, Aisha!" Bisa said, embracing her friend.

"Thank you for everything, my Sister," Aisha replied, returning the embrace.

Without further words, Aisha and Victoria got into Aisha's hidden copter and started for the city. Aisha said, "I really appreciate you for helping me. Now, I have to take you to the authorities. They will need to start asking you questions. They can also get you settled in a temporary home until we can all decide where you will best fit in. I promise that you will be treated with great respect and consideration."

"I understand. I expected worse."

Aisha called Nzinga and had Jomo arrange for officials from the security and hospitality departments to meet them at her house. She embraced and thanked Victoria again and watched as they left. She then went into her bedroom and collapsed on her own bed.

## Homecoming

Later that day, after Aisha had rested, she was summoned to an emergency meeting of the Council to give a report. "Wow!" she thought, "Word got around quickly."

As she walked out of her house, she saw that Nzinga, Amma, Aset and Fumi were waiting outside. Nzinga spoke, "We cannot discuss any details in advance of the Council session but need to know that you are alright."

"I am fine, thank you. Where is Victoria?"

"She is undergoing preliminary debriefing. I am to speak to her after the Council meeting," said Amma.

"Please contact Jay or another trusted Loyalist to witness her taking a Blood Oath that she is not a spy and mean us no harm as soon as possible," Aisha said.

"Done," Aset said. "That was the first thing Jay said to do. He also added that she would be perfectly honest in all her spoken words and answers. She took the Oath without question or hesitation."

"Next question. How are my brothers?"

"Fumi spoke up, "They are very upset at us and with you. But they'll get over it. Jomo has smoothed the way, and you know they can't stand up to Mama Nzinga."

They all laughed at this truism and proceeded to walk to the Council chambers, which were only a few blocks from Aisha's home.

When Nzinga and the Omowale ladies entered the Council building, Obadele and Kwame rushed up to Aisha. Obadele said, "I don't know whether to hug you or fuss at you. That was so reckless. You could have been hurt, killed or worse."

Kwame said nothing but embraced his sister tightly. They all went into the Chambers. Fumi went in also since she had been summoned as a participant in the plan.

Jomo opened the session with the usual, "Agoo"!

The attendees replied, "Amee," and took their seats.

Jomo said, "It is not appropriate at this time to comment on the wisdom or risks of Aisha's mission. It is done. Please remember that I requested permission from this body, and you gave me your trust and your permission. All that is to be done now is to listen to Aisha's report and decide on our future actions. Aisha, come forward."

Aisha walked slowly to the podium. She had not prepared a report and was actually wondering what to say to the crowded chamber. She asked the Elders for permission to speak, and when this was granted, she said, "Hotep all!!" "Hotep," and the room thundered.

Aisha took a deep breath and began. She described the internal intrigue present in New Europa and how she felt that her visit was really a maneuver by Joshua to flush out his opposition. She described her impression of his injuries but admitted that she did not actually see him after the assassination attempt. She informed them that his recovery was estimated at five to six weeks, so she was told, but still couldn't be sure of the truthfulness of this prediction. Aisha estimated that the unrest caused by the attempt on her and Joshua's lives probably meant that the coming offensive would likely be delayed, which gave Humanity more opportunity to prepare.

She described Joshua's compound stressing the domed enclosure. She gave her impression of the violence and the casual manner that it was dispensed. She described the presence of Loyalists, described to her by Victoria all over Europa, who were tired of the economic inequality and the brutality of the military. Victoria had emphasized that there were Loyalists armed and ready to support any Human military action. Aisha finally gave her opinion that in order to neutralize the Horde and provide long-lasting security for Humanity, lessons from the eighteenth Kemetic dynasty might become necessary. Invasion of Europa in order to control the borders, an offensive defense.

When she finished, she noticed that ninety minutes had passed. Her family all had solemn facial expressions. Amma summed up the situation, "We have a lot of work to do."

# ABOUT THE AUTHOR

Burnett Kwadwo Gallman is an eternal student with many interests. As a physician, he is focused on the health and welfare of all humanity and especially eradicating racial health disparities. As an amateur historian, he has studied, taught, lectured, and written on topics as varied as ancient Kemetic (Egyptian) history and culture, medieval West Afrikan history and Ausa (Afrikans from the United States of America) history and culture.

As a science fiction buff, he has enjoyed reading the works of Walter Mosley and Harlan Ellison. As a former musician, he has amassed a large collection of vinyl albums, cassette tapes and CD's of jazz, R & B, gospel, Afrikan music and drumming, and European classical music. As an amateur genealogist, he has researched his family history, tracing his paternal line to 18th century Angola.

As a race man, he has studied, lectured and written on such varied topics as Agnotology, Epigenetics, and Afrikan-centered Rites of Passage. This work is the result of the influence and urging of his late friend, Listervelt Middleton (Maa Kheru) and is an attempt to marry some of his interests.